DAMIEN

FEDERAL PROTECTION AGENCY

BOOK SIX

BY EVIE RILEY

DAMIEN

FEDERAL PROTECTION AGENCY

BOOK SIX

COPYRIGHT © 2023

EVIE RILEY

SECOND EDITION

ISBN: 978-1-77357-671-8

PUBLISHED BY NAUGHTY NIGHTS PRESS LLC

COVER ART BY WILLSIN ROWE

DAMIEN

It takes three to make life go right...

Private Investigator Damien Anderson and his younger brother watched in horror as their parents were killed in cold blood by the head of the mafia. Eye witnesses to a crime boss suspected in multiple homicides and a major gun trafficker, they have spent the last fifteen years in the Witness Protection program.

A teddy bear at heart, Damien can be sweet and kind but the moment anyone puts the people he loves at risk, he has no problem becoming lethal. Working with the FPA, the brothers find themselves at a crossroads when their past starts to catch up to them. Do they tell the men in the Agency the truth, or run once more and leave behind everyone they've come to think of as family?

Ex FBI Agent Max Morris is a man with a darker personality and a deadly skill set, who just happens to be the very definition of vigilante justice... and he has no issue with admitting it. Fed up with tracking down some of the worst repeat offenders only for the court to let them go on technicalities, Max quit the FBI and took matters into his own hands. He doesn't regret a moment of it. Someone has to take the predators like his father off the street.

Travis Manning is a social worker and the newest member of the FPA task force. He is in his element helping to find safe haven homes for the children in need. The shy, secretive, non-social man suffers from low self-esteem, which isn't helped when he seems to always end up dating men who are in the closet and keep him as their dirty secret. Travis always feels like he isn't good enough, until he's caught between Max and Damien. Literally.

When Travis' abusive ex shows up in Baton Rouge and proves he's a risk to the sweet man they love, what lengths will Max and Damien go to in order to keep Travis safe forever?

CHAPTER ONE

Travis

I WAS LATE. I knew he was going to be mad, but there was nothing I could do about it. Isaiah had to talk to me about the Agency needing one of us in Baton Rouge. He didn't order me, he couldn't, but I knew he was hoping that I would volunteer to leave. To move away from Gaithersburg and go to Baton Rouge.

EVIE RILEY

I had never lived in a large city. I'd never had much of a desire to do it. When I got my degree in Social Work, I wanted to work in a smaller town so I could build stronger connections with the children who were in my caseload. I didn't want to have a caseload of a hundred children and have to try and keep track of that many. I knew that Social Workers with a lot of children in their caseload, well, they lose track of children. They can't spend the time needed with each child to ensure they are safe and happy. That's when things can fall through the cracks, children can fall through the cracks, and that wasn't something I ever wanted to have happen on my watch.

I knew it would be between Isaiah and myself when it came down to who made the transfer, but I also knew that Isaiah had his own life in Gaithersburg. He had his boyfriend and other responsibilities so he couldn't move. It made the most sense for me to move, but what Isaiah didn't know, what everyone didn't know, was that I had a boyfriend. He was in the closet and he held zero interest in coming out of it. I had to respect that. I wasn't in a position to try and give him an ultimatum. Even if I told him he had to come out or I leave him, I knew I would be leaving him. He would never choose me over his reputation. That was something I had accepted, begrudgingly, sure, but I had accepted it years ago.

We had been dating for three years now, and in the beginning, it was all really great. We had met at a gay bar a couple of towns away. I knew he was from Gaithersburg, I had seen him around town. I had no idea he was gay and living in the closet, not until I saw him that night.

I'd never expected to see Detective Joe Baxter in a gay bar. He always came across as an old fashioned man with old fashioned beliefs. He certainly never gave any indication in the few dealings we'd had when I was working with a child in the system. Even when I was brought in because a twelve year old boy's parents were abusing him because he was gay, Baxter never gave any indication that he sympathized with the boy. He very much saw the parents' point of view and he didn't believe in being gentle with the boy.

There were simply no tells. He never let anyone know he was gay. Ever.

I knew Dr. Howard would tell me that Baxter hated himself because he was gay and until he loved and accepted himself fully, he would never be able to have a true and meaningful relationship. At the time, though, I didn't believe that. I believed, foolishly, that I could change him. And now, after three years of dating in secret, my life was no longer my own.

"You're late. Where the fuck have you been?" Baxter demanded the second I walked through the door.

We didn't live together, but he was always over at my place. He would use the fire escape around the back and sneak in that way so no one would see him coming through the front door. It was one of his rules.

He had a lot of rules.

The most important one was that no one in the town could know he was gay. He didn't acknowledge me in public. Even when we were in a different town for a date, there were no public displays of affection. No hand holding, no pet names, nothing. As far as any of the onlookers were concerned, we were friends out for a meal or we were having a business meeting.

At first, I was okay with it. I was younger and had never had a serious relationship before. And with my parents not being affectionate, I wasn't really used to being hugged or shown any affection to begin with. Not having any from Baxter was just normal for me. Now after three years, I was getting very tired. I was lonely and considering I didn't go to bed alone, that screamed volumes.

Baxter, he was rough in the bedroom and outside of it. Even our sex was hard and controlling. He never gave me oral sex. In fact, he almost never touched me. We always had sex in one position, doggy style, because he didn't want to see me. His actual words. He needed to be able to pretend that he wasn't having sex with a guy. His self-hatred was far deeper than I thought it was and it wasn't until I already had feelings invested into him and our relationship did I discover how deep it went.

I also discovered he had anger issues that could result in him hitting me. I should have left after the first time he hit me, but I had believed his lies when he said it wouldn't happen again. When he told me he didn't mean to, he had been drinking too much, that he was under a lot of pressure at work, I shouldn't have believed him, but I was a fool and forgave him.

Now, I had to wear long sleeved shirts and pants every day to make sure no one noticed the bruises that littered my body from him. He would even hit me now during sex if his anger started to boil over. He wasn't angry at me, but at himself. I was just his punching bag.

I knew I had to get out, but I honestly didn't know how. He had already told me he would kill me if I left him. I wasn't certain if he would, but with a town this small, he could easily do it. Plus he was a detective. He could make it look like an accident or that I killed myself. I didn't really have friends in town and my parents had checked out a long time ago, so I knew no one would even think twice about my death.

"I'm sorry, Isaiah needed to speak with me after work about the new group home project that we are working on," I said as I went and hung up my coat.

I was really hoping he would be okay with my excuse. I knew he was getting annoyed by all of the hours I had been working. It had been a problem since I had agreed to work with the Federal Protection Agency. Baxter didn't like that I had to travel now and that I wasn't there to fulfill his needs on demand.

Before the Agency, I was home every night to make dinner and make sure my place was clean before he came over. Now, I had been so busy that things had slipped. I wasn't always here with dinner cooked when he arrived. I wasn't always in the mood to have sex, either. He wasn't pleased with that.

I had a protein deficiency that made me tire easily. It also made me bruise easier and I had a harder time gaining weight. It's why I was so thin, something that I knew could be a turn off. It wasn't that I didn't eat, I just couldn't gain weight like everyone else so I was thin. I was only a hundred and twenty pounds and at five foot eight, that meant my ribs were easy to feel.

I knew some guys liked spinners, but I also knew that a lot of guys were turned off by someone being so thin. I couldn't help it, though, just like I couldn't help being tired most of the time, or the random bruises that I would get. It also made me have a weaker immune system and with being around kids, I tended to get sick often. It was just another thing that made it harder for me to have a real relationship. No one wanted to date the sick guy. My own parents didn't want to deal with my health. I couldn't exactly expect that there would be a man out there who would tolerate it.

The sudden blow to my stomach was unexpected and strong enough to knock me down to my knees and take my breath away.

"How many times do I really have to tell you that I don't give a shit about your excuses. When you are not out of town, you are home with dinner ready for when I get here. Your only job is to please me and recently, all you have done is prove to me what a worthless piece of shit you truly are. It's no surprise that your own parents don't love you."

His words hurt more than any punch could ever hurt. Baxter knew that, though. He knew how to hurt me, how to truly hurt me. He knew that I felt insecure and had low self-esteem from growing up, and he always made sure to let me know how worthless I was.

As if I needed someone to remind me.

"I'm sorry, I didn't realize how late it had gotten," I instantly apologized. I knew it wouldn't matter, though. He would only see it as me giving him excuses.

His right hand was instantly in my hair and pulling a chunk of it as hard as he could. He then wrapped his left hand around my throat, choking me. He pulled me up and slammed my back against the wall.

I brought my hands up to clutch at his arm, to try and get his hand off my neck. He was gripping it so tight, I wasn't able to breathe. He had never choked me before. In the bedroom from behind while he drove his cock into my ass, yes, but it was never anything like this. Never to the point where I was unable to breathe. The look in his eyes was pure darkness, pure hatred and anger. Something must have happened at work to push him over the edge today, and I was the one who would be paying for it.

"How many times do I have to tell you that I don't want to hear any excuses coming from your mouth? Your excuses mean nothing to me. You mean nothing to me. Your job is to cook, clean, and be there for when I need to fuck someone. That is all you are good for. You don't get to talk, all you get to do is apologize for being a disappointment." Another blow to my side, landing right where my healing bruises from the last fight we had were. "Now, take your punishment like the good worthless whore that you are," he seethed.

Before my brain could even register what was happening, Baxter had thrown me to the floor and had started to pull my pants down.

***

Two Weeks Later....

I placed the last box down on the floor in my new bedroom.

This was still so surreal to me. I had never expected that I would be moving to Baton Rouge, but this was where my job had brought me. I had been working in Social Services in Gaithersburg since right after I graduated College, close to five years now. I enjoyed working there. I liked being in a smaller town, getting to know the people and building connections with the kids that I had in my charge.

Now, unbelievably, I was going to work in Baton Rouge.

A city with over two hundred thousand people and a crime rate that could give New York City a run for its money. Daunting didn't even begin to explain how it felt. I was excited, though. I'd desperately needed the change.

When the Federal Protection Agency had moved here, I'd understood why. It made complete sense for them to be in a larger city that could accommodate all of the new Agents. Plus, the city was very high in the sex trade and most were underage children who were either runaways or kidnapped victims. The Agency was very much needed there.

With the move of the Agency though, Isaiah and myself had been very busy with having to travel all around the country with them. It was getting to be a lot and we were having a very difficult time with trying to find safe places for the victims that were rescued to go to. Isaiah had been working with Dominic to build a group home that we could use for the victims that we couldn't find a safe home for right away, but it was slow going.

When Mason had informed us that he needed one of us to be down here, to move down here, I knew it would be me. Isaiah was madly in love with his boyfriend, Sol, and Sol's younger brother, River. They all lived together and River was attending a private school for exceptionally gifted children. They had a whole life together in Gaithersburg now, a family, and it wouldn't be fair to make them all uproot their lives. Besides, it was the excuse that I needed to get away. The justification I had been waiting for to finally leave Baxter. He had made the decision for me after that horrible night, and it truly was a night I would never forget.

The bruises still littered my body from what he had done to me that night. When he'd finished the many rounds of sex with me, he'd finally left. We'd had had rough sex plenty of times in the past, hell, it was the only type of sex that we had.

That night, though, that night was different.

Normally, he would stretch me a bit first and he would use lube, but that night he didn't. He'd forced his way into me and he didn't care that he had made me bleed. That he'd really hurt me.

Afterward, I couldn't fool myself into

believing that it was sex anymore. No matter how hard I tried, my mind refused to allow me to accept that it was just sex. Looking back now, that was probably a good thing. It made me finally realize the truth.

He had raped me.

My own boyfriend had raped me. He'd beaten me and raped me. And then, he left me there in a mess of blood and cum, lying on the floor like I was nothing. I knew I couldn't do it anymore. I had taken a shower and called Isaiah and told him I would be happy to make the move to Baton Rouge.

From there, I spent the next two weeks trying to avoid Baxter and getting my apartment packed up. I couldn't pack it until I was ready to leave. I had to make sure Baxter didn't know I was leaving, because I truly believed he would kill me to keep me quiet. That he wasn't going to risk me talking about him being in the closet.

I had boxes stored under my bed and hidden in the back of the closet so Baxter wouldn't see them. Then the night before I left, I was up all night packing everything up and loading it in a rented U-Haul truck and I left for Baton Rouge in the very early morning hours.

I had gotten a whole new phone with a new number and made sure to give it to Isaiah so he would have it. I had to disappear as far as Baxter was concerned. If he didn't know where I was, then I wouldn't have to worry about him trying to find me. He would have no reason to ask about me at work or ask Isaiah where I was. At least, not without him risking people wondering why he cared about my whereabouts.

Baton Rouge was going to be my fresh start. It was going to be the time that I needed to try and recover from Baxter and the abuse, and from my parents. I was twenty-seven, I shouldn't feel like this. I shouldn't feel like I was worthless and unimportant. I had to figure out how to heal, otherwise I was never going to be able to not only love myself, but someone else.

I wanted to have a real relationship someday. I wanted to know what it felt like to truly be loved and cherished, but that was never going to be possible if I couldn't love myself first. If I wasn't able to see my own self-worth.

I had a lot that I needed to work on internally, emotionally and psychologically, but I was hoping that being in Baton Rouge and having my own space again, I would be able to start to mend from everything. This was my new life, my new home, and I was determined to make the most of it.

CHAPTER TWO

Damien

"RACHEL'S STALKING CASE has been closed. The guy is sitting pretty in jail now," Sebastian said as he walked into my office and plopped down in the chair across from my desk.

"Did he give you any trouble?"

Rachel had been a new client of our private investigation agency. I knew

Mason wanted us to work exclusively for him and the Federal Protection Agency, but I was not about to let the company that Sebastian and I had built dissolve. We had men who worked for us and they were relying on the work to feed themselves and their families.

We used to be located in Gaithersburg, but with the FPA utilizing our skills so often, it made sense for us to move down to Baton Rouge. We had clients all over the country and with being in a larger city now, we were getting more local clients.

Rachel had been dealing with a stalker for two years now, but the police hadn't done anything about it. It wasn't their fault per say, they could only do so much, and Rachel's stalker had made sure to stay within the terms of the restraining order. That didn't change the fact that he was still stalking her and terrorizing her.

"Nope, he fell right into the trap and he is now facing ten years in prison. Rachel is going to use this opportunity to relocate to California where her sister lives. You got something else for me?"

"Not yet. Mason is on his way over here to talk about something with me. They might have something that they need help with."

"He didn't say what it was?"

"Nope."

We had done plenty of cases with the FPA since it was created. Both Sebastian and I enjoyed the work and we were always willing to help someone, should they need it. We wanted to help make this world a safer place for the current generation and the future ones. If it involved children, there was nothing we wouldn't do, and I do mean *nothing*.

We had both killed someone before and hidden the body. Hell, I had done that within the past six months when Isaiah called me when his boyfriend Sol's younger brother had been kidnapped. I arrived on scene to find the kidnapper dead, by his own son's doing.

Max Morris was just standing there completely calm, as if he didn't just shoot his father to death. We had buried the body and had covered it all up with the help of Mason.

It had helped to know that Max's father, Phillip, was a pedophile who had not only molested and raped children, but he had killed them as well. He deserved to be killed and it was one time I'd had no problem covering it up.

"Any news on Russo?" Sebastian

asked.

David Russo.

That man had been a thorn in both of our sides for fifteen years now. People knew that Sebastian and I were best friends. That we grew up together and started this company together. We kept our personal lives pretty quiet and only told people what they needed to know.

What people didn't know, though, was that it was mostly all a lie.

We did grow up together and we were best friends, but we were also brothers. Sebastian was my kid brother. We had always been close growing up. We grew up in New Jersey with a big loving family. We were full blooded Italians so there was always a family gathering with close to a hundred people there for it. Every month, someone in the family held a family dinner for everyone. Our mother didn't work, but our father was an accountant for a major corporation. At least, that's what we were told.

We grew up rich, we never went without, and anything we wanted, we got. On our sixteenth birthday, we were both given a brand new Dodge Charger. Birthdays we had a huge celebration and would receive easily five thousand dollars worth of gifts. Christmas was even worse.

For two decades, I thought my family was perfect, that we were always going to have each other. That was, until I was twenty. Sebastian and I had been off on a vacation in Europe. We were not set to come home for a few more days, but there was a major storm coming into New Jersey and we had been worried about our parents. We wanted to be home to make sure they were safe and if they needed to be evacuated, we would be there to make sure they went.

When we had arrived no one was home, but we were exhausted from jetlag so we headed up to our rooms and crashed for a few hours. I woke up to Sebastian shaking me four hours later. I figured our parents had finally gotten home, and they had, but they were also with David Russo and some of his thugs.

Everyone in New Jersey knew who David Russo was. He was the head of the Italian mob in the State. He was a fifty year old man who was known for being cruel and deadly. No one crossed him and if they did, they did so knowing that it would result in their death.

At the time, we had no idea why Russo would be speaking with our parents. Just as we were about to go downstairs to ask what was going on, Russo's thugs pulled out their guns and shot both of our parents. Killing them execution style.

I'd had just enough reflex within me to grab Sebastian, cover his mouth with my hand and pull him back into my bedroom.

Even thinking about it now, I could feel my heart racing. That was the night that I first felt true fear. We both did. Up until that point, we had never felt terror; we never had the need to. Seeing our own parents being executed was not something either one of us could forget.

I had taken Sebastian into my room and we hid in the closet. It would have been funny considering we had always been out and proud; if it hadn't been for the fact that we had to hide from the men who killed our parents. We hid for close to an hour, waiting to see if someone knew we were here, but when no one came looking for us, we ventured out.

We found them right where they had died in the living room and Russo and his guys were gone. We had called the police and the Feds came. We both agreed to testify and we were immediately placed in witness protection. We testified against Russo and he went away for a double homicide. He was sentenced to life, and Sebastian and I were sentenced to a life of being hidden.

We had foolishly thought that when Russo was sentenced to life in prison that meant we would get to be free from the witness protection program. That we could go back to our lives like it never even happened.

We were sorely mistaken.

The threat against our lives didn't stop with Russo in jail, it got worse.

We were taken back into WitSec and spent the next five years moving around. The Agent who had been put on as our protector was killed five years in.

We had always suspected that Russo had someone working for the Feds and that mole gave up our location. After that, we spent the next ten years relocating ourselves and constantly changing our names and appearances. Gaithersburg was supposed to be a quick stop, but we ended up liking the place and the people that we came across. Now, we were in our first major city in fifteen years and we were on even more of a high alert than usual.

We both wanted this to end. We both wanted to be able to feel safe and not have to look over our shoulders. We had been investigating ourselves. Trying to figure out who Russo's hit men were so we could take them out before they got to us. It wasn't an easy process, though, and so far, we had only managed to take out two. We knew there were at least a dozen, if not more, but with each one that we took out they got smarter and it got harder to find them. We would get them, but I wasn't confident that would be before they found us again.

"Nothing yet. We got feelers out, all we can do is wait and see what comes up," I answered.

"Maybe no news is good news in this case. Do any of the guys need any help with what they are working on?"

"Nothing has come up yet."

"And our newest member, where is

he?"

Max Morris.

There was a new pain in my ass. I had not been planning on hiring him, especially after that whole Phillip fiasco, but against my better judgment, I did. I was hoping that maybe he just needed a place where he could call home, have brothers around him.

I did look into him. I knew he used to be a Federal Agent before he left to hunt down his father. With his father now dead, I figured he would calm back down.

Turns out, the man preferred vigilante work over letting the justice system handle it.

He was careful, very careful, I had to give him that. But I knew, eventually, his luck was going to run out and it was either going to be a bullet or a prison cell that got him. Both options bothered me and I wasn't truly certain why.

We were polar opposites in a lot of ways. He had no problem killing in cold blood, as long as the one on the other end was a criminal. I only killed if lives were on the line. There was a difference and Max didn't seem to have that moral compass like most human beings do.

"Fuck if I know, which isn't a good thing."

"I'm surprised you have been keeping him around. You don't like wild cards, and Max is the very definition of a wild card."

"I keep hoping he calms down. We've both come across guys who are like him and all they needed was someone to show them the right way. To give them a family. Maybe Max needs the same."

"Maybe, but I would keep a close eye on him, if I were you," Sebastian warned before he stood up.

Just as he made it to the door, Mason strode in. Mason offered us both a small smile as Sebastian nodded at him and headed out.

"I hope I'm not interrupting anything," Mason said as he slipped into the chair that Sebastian had just vacated.

"Not at all. Sebastian just wrapped up a case. What can I do for you?"

"I am hoping you will be able to take on a security assessment gig. It's local and there aren't any immediate threats. You would be assessing a situation to see about any potential threats and then helping to prevent them from happening."

"Okay, I'm gonna need more information than that." I chuckled.

DAMIEN

We had run threat assessments before and it was easy work. Mason paid well so this would be an easy payday for me. We all worked our own cases and we got the pay associated with that case. Sebastian and I used some of our pay to keep the lights on, but my guys didn't have to worry about any overhead expenses. It also helped to give my guys the incentive to bring in new clients. It was working and since we had been helping with the Agency, we had both been able to make pretty decent money. Money that would come in handy should we have to leave at a moment's notice once again.

"As you know, the safe havens in the foster home system are being restructured. Travis is reworking the whole system. He is going to have new safe havens constructed from older homes. It would help to have someone within the security world to go with him and run the threat assessment so the city can implement the needed changes to the structures. You would go with him to the different homes and run the threat assessment. At the same time, though, you would also be working as protection. Some of the areas that Travis is going into are dangerous and they might not take it too kindly to a Social Worker poking around."

To say the least.

Most of the gangs in town didn't like Social Workers or first responders of any kind. It was part of their society and that was something we all had to accept. They didn't care for my guys either, because we worked with the Agency. If some of them knew that Travis was poking around to get ideas for the new safe havens, they might take matters into their own hands to stop him. A lot of gang members weren't happy about the safe havens because the children who were being kept safe within them were snitches against them.

"That's fine. I'll handle it. When is he going to get started?"

"On Monday. I can have him text you the information."

"Works for me."

"Thank you. I really appreciate it. My guys are spread thin right now. We got case requests coming out of our ass."

"Better than nothing coming in. We're happy to help, you know that."

I knew they were getting busier. Mason had to bring on more guys for the field and for the computer tech stuff. It was good, though, it meant they were solving more cases and helping more children. That in and of itself was worth all of the long hours.

"I appreciate it. You guys have been saving my ass for a while now. Couldn't do it without you," he said, flashing a warm smile as he stood.

"Sounds good. Be safe," I said.

"Same for you and your brother," he said with a smirk.

"He's not my brother," I instantly countered.

"Sure," he said with a knowing smile as he headed out.

"Son of a bitch," I said softly to myself once I was alone.

I knew Mason was smart. Both him and his brother, Roland. Neither of them had believed us when we said we were just best friends. They both knew it was a lie.

Sebastian and I don't look identical, but you could clearly tell we had the same facial characteristics. Most of the time, we could play it off as a weird coincidence, but every now and then, we came across someone who didn't buy our story. It would appear that Mason and Roland really didn't believe us, and they obviously knew that something more was going on. Thankfully, they both seemed perfectly happy to live in our lie and not demand answers. Though, that could be because they both knew we wouldn't be able to give them. Still, Mason letting me know that he knew was his way of making sure I knew that he had our back. That should there ever come a day when we needed their help, he would be there.

That was something that Sebastian and I had this time around compared to the other towns over the past fifteen years. We had friends who were more than capable of handling themselves in a dangerous situation. I just hoped we would never have to ask them for help. That we would never have to ask them to put their lives on the line for us. With some luck, that day might never come and Sebastian and I could finally live our lives in peace without having to constantly look over our shoulders waiting for the next attack to happen. We could have a boyfriend and settle down without having to be ready to pack up and leave at a moment's notice. Maybe one day. Hopefully.

CHAPTER THREE

Max

"COME ON, YOU son of a bitch," I said as I peered through my scope.

I had been trying to get this bastard for a couple of days now, but so far he hadn't moved into a position that would give me a clean shot. This had to be clean. I was only going to get one shot at this without anyone noticing.

Matt Wentworth, an unconvicted child molester.

His latest victim was a six year old little boy that he'd raped. The boy was so traumatized that he had stopped speaking, and by the time he was found in an abandoned warehouse, the evidence was completely gone. It fit Wentworth's MO, though, and the police had him on camera speaking with the boy, but they never had anything concrete that they could use to convict him. The other times he was arrested for child molestation, the cases had been dropped because the children refused to testify and the parents couldn't bring themselves to force them.

It was a common occurrence in the justice system. Victims being too afraid to speak up and testify. To sit in an open court filled with strangers and tell them what had happened to them. To talk about being violated with the person that had done it to you sitting right there not even ten feet from you. Nope. The kids were simply too afraid. The justice system was seriously flawed and we would have more victims willing to speak up and testify if they didn't have to go through something so public and humiliating. And that was before you factored in the defense attorney who loved nothing more than to make the defendant feel like the victim. To turn it all around on the victim and have everyone believe that they asked for it or they were having second thoughts afterward and thought they should try and cover it up. Or it was a custody battle and mom was just crying child molestation to keep dad away from the kids. It was all bullshit and often the offender got to walk away and attack the next person.

Pedophiles and rapists, they don't just stop at one. They liked to keep going until they got caught, and even if they did get jail time, when they got out they went right back to it. There is no cure for that kind of scum. There is no set amount of time where they could be locked up and rehabilitated that would make an honest to goodness change in them. There was no changing them, period. They were hard wired to violence, to those sexual urges. They didn't have that little voice in their head telling them not to touch that child. They didn't have any impulse control and they would always act on their urges. If the justice system wasn't going to lock them up for life, then someone had to be there to make sure they didn't get to keep violating people.

And I was more than happy to be that person.

I knew from personal experience that pedophiles never changed. I grew up with one in my home. I was just a kid when my own father started to touch me, started to rape me. By the time I was sixteen, I had grown too old for him and he left me alone. I should have been thankful, I guess, but the damage had already been done. I knew, though, that I wanted to be a Federal Agent, that I wanted to help put people like him behind bars, even if I couldn't bring myself to put *him* in jail. I became an FBI Agent and spent years chasing down criminals. Doing everything I could to make sure the bad guys ended up in prison where they belonged. I had also been keeping track of my father, making sure nothing was going on with him.

Even when I discovered that he was a foster parent, I didn't do anything. I should have, I knew that, but my own trauma kept me afraid of him. It kept me from being able to move on and take action. I hated myself for it.

I had discovered that I was gay when I was eighteen and in the FBI Academy. I hadn't even noticed up until that point, and discovering that I was attracted to men after being raped by my own father for years, had caused a serious identity issue inside me.

It took a long time before I was able to accept that I was gay and that even though I was attracted to men, that didn't mean I wanted my father to do those things, that I enjoyed it. It took even longer before I was able to allow another man to touch me. Still, it was always there. He always stood in the way of me being able to find peace and move on from what he had done to me. I knew I was never going to be able to start to heal until I finally got justice for myself.

It was in that moment of clarity that I knew what I needed to do. I left the FBI and I started to follow my father around the country. He moved around a lot so he could continue to be a foster parent and abuse the children without it getting out. There were only so many times a single male could take in young pre-pubescent boys before it started to look suspicious. The trick with my father was, though, he didn't beat them or neglect them. He took very good care of them. He made them feel like they had everything to lose if they told anyone about what he was doing.

That's what he'd done with Sol and River.

He never touched River, he was too young at the time, but he did with Sol. He made sure Sol knew just how lucky they were to be with him. He made sure River had everything he could ever want and as long as Sol continued to allow my father to rape him, River would never know what it felt like to be hurt. My father knew exactly how to play things.

It wasn't until a couple of years after I started tracking him did I discover that he was also going after runaways and killing them. I didn't know that he could be violent. He had never been violent with me or with any of his other victims after me. He seemed to have everything figured out and had a perfect system to not get caught. It was a shock to discover he had been killing his victims. The ones that he couldn't ensure would never talk. Runaways were easy targets but they were also impossible to control. They didn't live under his roof, they could easily tell someone what had happened to them. It didn't have to be a cop or a doctor, it could be a friend, a priest, someone working in a soup kitchen. There was no telling who that person could tell. The only way my father would be able to ensure that his victim didn't talk would be to kill them afterward. After all, if a runaway doesn't get found, police just assume they fled to a different town or were good at hiding. They didn't look too hard for them.

I had every intention of killing my father when Sol and River were in his care, but before I could, all three disappeared. I knew Sol and River had run away and my father was trying to find them. I started to follow them as well, knowing that eventually, my father would pop up. He wasn't going to tolerate them getting away from him. He couldn't report them missing either, because that would lead to too many questions once they were found. My father couldn't risk Sol talking to the police.

I had followed them for years with the hope that my father would show up. I was still trying to keep track of his movements, but they were harder to follow. He was no longer getting children from the foster care and relying on runaways to fulfill his sick needs. When I had overheard that Sol and River would be heading into Gaithersburg, I headed there myself, never expecting that it would change all three of our lives.

When my father had kidnapped River, I knew what he was planning to do to him. I was not going to let the opportunity to finally get my own justice slip through my fingers. Not again. Getting to that motel, being able to look him in the eyes as I held that gun on him, getting to pull the trigger and watch as his life left his body...

There was no greater feeling.

I was finally able to feel peace.

It didn't even matter that I had killed him in front of witnesses or in broad daylight. It didn't matter that I could be going to jail for murder, it would all have been worth it. Every single second would have been worth the level of peace his death had finally brought to me.

Surprisingly enough, I didn't end up in jail. Damien had come into my life and he had helped me to cover it all up. He had managed to convince Mason to let it go and grant me immunity for the kill. I figured that would be it. I never figured that Damien would also make an offer for me to work in his private investigation business.

I had worked a few jobs for him and for the Agency when they needed it. When I didn't have a lead that was. Killing my father only helped me to realize that there were more like him out in the world. More pedophiles who were able to continue to rape and molest children because the justice system was failing them. I was in a position to be able to do something to stop them.

To give their victims some justice.

So whenever I got a lead and it was solid, I would go and take care of it. I would kill them and bring justice and peace to their victims and protect any future ones from being harmed by them. I had zero regrets about it. Someone had to protect the children and I would step up and do what had to be done without a single ounce of reluctance or feelings of guilt.

Every. Single. Time.

My phone vibrated in my pocket and I moved carefully to grasp it without jiggling my rifle around.

Where are you?

I couldn't contain the eye roll at seeing Damien's text. I didn't work full-time for him. I was free to come and go whenever I'd like as long as I wasn't working a case or helping with the Agency. I didn't think that meant he would be trying to keep tabs on me all of the time. I was free to do whatever I wanted and I didn't have to run it by him first.

He knew that I went after people on my own. He called me a vigilante, but that wasn't what I considered myself to be. I was just a guy utilizing his skills to get predators off of the streets. To help give justice to some victims and prevent additional victims in the future.

I sent him a text back telling him that I would be back in a couple of days. I was confident that I would be able to get my mark by then and I would head right back to Baton Rouge. I was going to need the money from another case if I wanted to keep paying my rent. I wasn't charging anyone for my services. I wasn't a hit man. I was simply doing this world a civic duty.

Once I got back to town, I could go and see Damien and find out what he wanted. Until then, I didn't have to worry about what he wanted or having to answer to him. He wasn't my boss and he wasn't about to be. I didn't need anyone in my corner. I didn't need to be a part of some misfit family like he had going over there, or like the guys in the Agency. I was perfectly fine on my own and that was how I was going to keep it. That's how I liked it.

CHAPTER FOUR

Travis

I MADE MY way toward the first house that I was going to be checking out today. I had received the list of abandoned properties that the city owned and I was planning on checking out the houses that would be outside of the gang-infested areas.

I had no idea what condition some of

these properties would be in. Unfortunately, the listing only had the address and that was it. There were no photos or much detail about the property itself. I tried to do some research on the properties last night, but there wasn't much coming back on them. All I was able to pick up was what type of property it was, such as a house or an apartment complex. I wanted to avoid apartments or homes that had been turned into different apartments. I wanted the children to be able to have their own home. It would be easier for security purposes as well if we didn't have to try and worry about who else could be renting the same house.

What I wasn't made aware of until late last night, was that Damien was going to be accompanying me to each of the properties. He was going to be running a threat assessment on each home to see if it would be a viable option for a safe haven. I also knew that he would be there to ensure I didn't cross paths with anyone dangerous while I went into abandoned buildings.

There was nothing stopping the homeless or drug users from squatting in the properties. As a result, it could be dangerous for me to go into them completely unarmed and alone. I was a Social Worker, so I was not about to start carrying a gun with me. I didn't like them to begin with and I didn't even know how to shoot one. Having a bit of added protection would be nice.

I didn't know Damien on a personal level. I had heard of him from other Agents in the Agency and from Isaiah. I had never met him, though, nor had I ever shared a conversation with the man. From everything that I had heard, he sounded like a decent man who was serious about his work and passionate about his business. I couldn't fault a man for any of that.

I was hoping he would keep everything professional and not want to engage in small talk all day. That could be exhausting. It wasn't that I didn't enjoy a good conversation, it was that I didn't care to share personal information about myself. Isaiah had been trying for years now to come over to my place and I always had an excuse as to why he couldn't. Baxter never wanted anyone over at the apartment in case he decided to come by. He wasn't going to risk anyone even seeing him with me in case they thought we were together.

DAMIEN

To Baxter, being gay was the ultimate sin. He hated gay people and found them disgusting. However, if he ever wanted to feel true pleasure, he had to give in to his urges and have sex with a man. It was what made our interactions so violent and hostile. He had all of this self-hatred and self-disgust within him that he had to take it out on someone, and I was the only one he could take it out on.

I had grown used to keeping everything a secret. I had gotten used to making sure I chose my words carefully when I was around people so nothing ever slipped. It made conversations exhausting and I often found that they weren't worth all of the work and energy needed to bother. So with any luck, Damien would only want to focus on the job and nothing personal.

I pulled up to the first house and

turned my car off after parking. The area wasn't too bad. There were some older homes in the neighborhood that needed work, but people were living in them. The house that we were going to be looking at was very rundown and I suspected the outside didn't do the inside any justice at all. Honestly, I was surprised it was even still standing. It looked like a good gust of wind would knock it right over. I knew they were going to be in rough shape, they were homes that were abandoned and had gotten picked up by the city with the hope that one day they would do something with them. So far, no one had been interested in purchasing them and the city held zero interest in renovating them or turning them into a business to sell. They could be perfect for safe havens if we were able to renovate them so they would be safe and livable.

I saw Damien pull up and park. I climbed out of my car and made my way toward him. I couldn't help but look around to make sure I hadn't been followed. I knew it was silly. Baxter wouldn't know I was out this way and he would never ask about me. That would attract too much unwanted attention to him and he wouldn't risk people questioning if he was friends with me. I was safe, but I still felt like I was being watched. I was hoping that feeling would fade with time.

"Hey. Damien, right?" I said, once I was close enough.

"Morning, it's nice to finally meet you properly," he said as he held his hand out for me.

I easily took it and I couldn't help but

notice the warmth that I felt with just a single touch from him.

"It's nice to meet you," I said, doing my best to not stutter.

I pulled my hand back and started to head toward the house. He easily followed behind me and I could see him looking around. I knew he had to work security and a big part of that was taking in the neighborhood and area of the potential safe haven. We had to make sure it would be safe from outside threats for everyone living in it.

"So, what made you decide to move to Baton Rouge?" he asked as we headed inside.

"Isaiah wasn't in a position to move, so I offered to," I answered, trying to keep it short and simple. It also wasn't a lie, so it would be easier to keep track.

I didn't want everyone knowing about Baxter or that I had been in an abusive relationship. I didn't want to be seen as a victim. As the guy who everyone had to walk on eggshells around. I didn't want to be seen that way and I wasn't about to start fresh by having to carry around that baggage.

"How are you liking it so far?" he asked next.

"Um, it's good. You?" I asked, trying to get the attention off me.

"Yeah, it's a nice enough town. Bigger than what I'm used to. It's been a long time since I've lived in a town this size. Makes it easier to find clients, though."

I just gave a nod as I moved around the house and started to take notes on what would need to be fixed up. I would have to submit a rough estimate of what would be needed by the city to make these homes livable. That was going to be the trick. I knew the city wasn't going to want to hand over a great deal of money just to make foster homes. However, they were going to have to do something if they didn't want a repeat of what recently happened. At least I had the most recent tragedy on my side. That wasn't a good thing morally, but for getting the city to agree to hand over thousands of dollars, it helped to have the media still up in arms over the death of nine innocent children. If we were going to make this happen, we had to move fast to get the support money.

"What about your family? Any siblings, your parents still alive?" He asked after a few minutes.

"No siblings and my parents are alive."

Typically I would ask him the same question, but I didn't want to make small talk. I didn't want to do the first date questions. I wanted to keep this strictly professional.

"Did you move here alone? Or do you have a boyfriend?" he asked next.

"No," I said, perhaps too tightly.

I really didn't want to talk about my past relationships. Not that it was any of his business to begin with. We didn't know each other and it wasn't like I was trying to be his friend. I didn't need friends. At least, not right now. I had to settle into my new life first, and start to work on myself before I tried to bring other people into my life. Hopefully, he would be able to accept that.

He must have gotten the picture that I wasn't about to keep talking, because the questions stopped. I finished making my way around the house and I could see that Damien had explored the house as well and had noted a few things down on his pad of paper. I suspected it was entry points that could be weak spots. The trick was we had to make the place look like a normal home so it wouldn't attract unwanted attention. If we put bars on the windows, people would talk about it and wonder what the kids had done to be in a house this secure. A crucial part of safe havens was their anonymity. No one knew where they were located, so they couldn't hire someone to go in and kill one of the witnesses.

"Is it viable?" I asked Damien once we both returned to what I assumed was the living room area.

"Construction wise, it seems like it's

got solid bones. It needs a lot of work done on the inside. I think if we get bulletproof glass on all of the windows and add some locks to them they will be safe. The trick will be the front and rear doors. We will need to find some type of security door that doesn't come across as a security door. The neighborhood seems to be in decent shape. I'll run their names when I get back to the office and make sure there aren't any criminal connections in the surrounding homes. Pending that, I think it's viable."

"Perfect. I have two more places that I can see today and then more tomorrow. Is that good for you?"

"Lead the way," he said with a nod.

We both made our way out of the house and I locked it up before I got to my car. He was going to follow me in his. I was happy to hear that it would be a viable option if we could get the money to renovate the house. I would need his threat assessment and his approval for it, but if everyone in the area came back clean, I was confident I would have it.

Ideally, we needed five homes to start with to make sure everyone had a safe place to be and we didn't have too many children in one home. That was the problem with the current safe haven homes. There were anywhere between seven to a dozen children in each home. And with only one person watching and caring for that many children, it was too much. We needed to have enough homes so that we could get the numbers down to five children maximum, with two adults in the home. It was going to be a lot of work, but I knew it would all be worth it in the end. For now, we had one house pending and I needed to find four more.

CHAPTER FIVE

Damien

WALKING AWAY FROM Travis didn't feel right. I couldn't help but feel like I was missing something vital about him.

All day long, he had been a bit jumpy and he seemed to be waiting for something to happen. He was trying to hide it, but my trained eyes could see the internal struggle he was going through. It could have easily been a side effect of his job. He did go into people's homes and remove children that were not safe. It wasn't just the cases that he worked on for the Agency, he had his own cases that he needed to work for the city and there was no telling how violent some of those cases could be.

When someone was dealing with children and having to remove them from their parents, emotions ran hot. The parents could take their anger out on him. Travis would be an easy target for their anger at themselves or the situation. He also wasn't a very large guy, he was definitely on the smaller side, and that would make him an easier target for their rage.

He was thin and I couldn't help but wonder if he was eating properly or if his job was getting to him. I knew it could be hard to be a social worker who worked with children. I knew that Travis had been involved in multiple cases for the Agency and had seen some of the worst that humanity had to offer. Seeing children being abused and injured day in and day out would take a toll on anyone. It wouldn't be surprising if he had trouble sleeping or eating at times.

It did concern me, though, that he was so thin. It shouldn't have mattered to me, but I couldn't help it. He didn't come across as healthy. He seemed very nervous, anxious, and stressed, and it wasn't good for someone to live that way. I had tried to talk to him, but every attempt to get any type of personal details from him was shot down. He kept everything professional and it was clear he didn't trust me on any level.

I was used to not being trusted, though. There had been plenty of times when I met with someone and they were uncertain about me. Whether it was due to my appearance, or the fact that I was the new guy in a job.

I would eventually earn Travis' trust. It would take time, but I also knew that working together had a way of forging bonds with people. I would earn his trust and, hopefully, he would feel like he could talk to me about anything that he was feeling or what was going on with him.

I was oddly fascinated by him. He was a good looking man, even if he looked like he needed a few good meals into him. He seemed to care a great deal about children and he took his job very seriously. He came across as a man with a good heart and that only made him more attractive.

I arrived back at the office for the detective agency and I trudged down the hall toward my office, intending to get started running the names of the neighbors for the one potential safe home location. I figured since I was aware some of the guys were already out working on a case and I knew that Sebastian had gone over to the FPA to see if there was something he could help out with, I'd have some time alone to work on this case. I loved my brother, but Sebastian always got antsy when he didn't have anything to do and sometimes he got under my skin in his boredom so I was glad he'd gone over to the Agency today.

The second I walked into my personal office, I was instantly annoyed. Max was back from whatever he was doing. He was sitting in the extra chair in my office with his boots up on my desk as he sat back in the chair. He knew that it drove me insane when he put his dirty boots on my desk, when anyone did it. This man was driving my tolerance and he knew it.

I tried my best to be understanding with him, to be patient and open minded where his quirks were concerned. He was very rough around the edges and I was trying to calmly help to smooth them out. To get to know who he was at his core, but this man could make a nun swear.

I went over and pushed his boots off from my desk as I spoke. "Where the hell have you been?"

He actually rolled his eyes at me, like he was twelve, as he put his legs up on the chair next to him. "You're not my father. He's in the ground getting eaten by worms. You seem very confused by that."

It was a good thing I wasn't his father, because when I punched him in his pretty face it wouldn't be child abuse. This man was the definition of guarded, and I knew that, I did, but some days it was very hard to remember that his attitude was his armor and not just his shitty personality.

I knew he had been through a lot growing up. I knew he had seen horrific things from his time in the FBI and while he followed his father around the country. His own father had raped him repeatedly, and he had been through horrible things at a very young age and I knew that could screw anyone up. I knew he had problems. What happened to him growing up didn't magically disappear because he was an adult. It had to be dealt with before the trauma would be able to be healed.

Max's way of protecting himself, from keeping the world from getting too close to him, was his attitude. He wore it like an armor and it screamed leave me the fuck alone. He wasn't arrogant or cocky. He was just unapproachable. He constantly wore this *fuck you* face that made everyone want to avoid any type of conversation with him. Being close to Max was the equivalent of dry humping a cactus naked.

I was trying to remember that he had been traumatized. I was trying to work on getting through some of the walls that he had placed around himself. The problem was, they were reinforced steel that was about six inches thick. Nothing short of a bomb would make a dent in his walls. I had yet to find anything that we could connect with outside of possible work cases. Something that would be a starting point for us to have a normal conversation or normal interactions on a more personal level.

I didn't want him to feel like I was lecturing him all the time. I didn't want him to feel like he couldn't come to me if he needed to talk or needed help. I would love for him to be *one of the guys* here. To see the guys that he works around most days of the week as friends, as brothers. I wanted all of our guys to feel like they had a family and a home here. And that was something that Max desperately needed, even if he didn't think so.

"I employ you, I have the right to know when one of my employees takes off to without any notice," I countered as I sat down.

"I work for you part-time when you need the extra hands. Not really the same thing. I'm basically a contract worker, so I can come and go whenever I want. But you will be happy to hear that I am back in town and open for work."

"Open for money, you mean," I pointed out.

I knew what he was doing. He was only working when he needed money to keep paying his bills and to cover travel expenses. Once he had enough, he went off to hunt down his next target on his personal list. I wasn't legally an accessory to murder, but I knew if Mason discovered that I knew what Max was doing, he would stop utilizing me and my guys for their cases. If it had just been me and Sebastian, I wouldn't have thought much about it, but our guys relied on the money coming in from the FPA cases and I was not about to screw them out of something they needed for their families.

"Why else do people work?" he countered with a smirk.

"Some people do it because they want to make a difference in the world. You do know that you could be making a bigger difference if you worked full-time here or at the FPA. Compared to going out there and being a vigilante, at least."

It wasn't that I didn't understand why he did it. I truly did comprehend his reasons and the younger version of me would have been right there with him. I completely agreed that there were too many times when the justice system failed and dangerous criminals got to walk away scot free without suffering any punishment or injury. I completely agreed that those criminals deserved to be killed. That people who murdered, abused and molested children should automatically be sentenced to death and not allowed to languish on easy street in a jail cell. If anyone destroyed a child's life, they should have to pay for it with their own life. Yes, prison wasn't fun, but they were getting three meals a day, they could still work and make money, crappy money but money nonetheless, and they still had their lives. They could even use computers, get an education, get married, have sex, they could have a lot of luxuries that came with life.

Whereas if they lived through the horrible experiences done to them, some of their victims would never be able to function normally in society again. Some might never be able to tolerate being touched by another human being again. Others might never be able to leave their own home because of the trauma they experienced. It wasn't right that the evil people who did that to them got to live out the rest of their life comfortably.

Still, Max was putting himself in a dangerous position. He could potentially be arrested for murder and spend the rest of his life locked up. And then what would happen to all of the children out there who are waiting for someone to come through the door and save them from their hell. He wanted to make a difference, but he was going about it the wrong way and I had been trying to get him to see that for months now.

"So you have said. Look, I am careful and I cover my tracks. Besides, when the cops find the bodies it's not like they are going to be heartbroken and alert the media to seek justice for their death. No one cares when a monster gets put down."

"Monster or not, the detectives still have to solve their cases, regardless of who the victim is. Every time you go out there to kill someone, you are putting yourself at risk of being thrown in prison. How are you going to help people if that happens? How many children will you save then? You're not thinking about the long-term or seeing the bigger picture. All you can see is your father's face on every child molester, but your father is dead. You killed him, you don't need to keep killing him to help children."

And that was exactly it. The trauma was still too fresh in Max. He wasn't able to see anything but Phillip's face on each of his targets. He was still trying to get justice for himself and he was using surrogates to accomplish it. He needed time to process what happened to him growing up and the fact that he did kill his own father. He wasn't giving himself the time that he needed and I was worried it would get him killed one day.

"What I do with my time is none of your business," he said, with a deadly edge lacing his voice.

I had apparently pushed too hard today and I knew I was going to have to let it go for now. Thankfully, I had something we could talk about.

"We have a new case we're working. Travis, a Social Worker for the Agency, needs to create new safe havens after the last one was set on fire and killed nine children. Mason would like us to run security and threat assessments while the homes are being designed and built. I saw Travis today and we are meeting tomorrow for nine in the morning at a potential location. I'll text you the address."

He just gave a nod before he climbed to his heavily booted feet. I felt slightly surprised at the easy acquiesce. I figured he would have given me some excuse about him not doing a case this simple. It seemed like Max needed money more than I thought he did. It worked well in my favor, though, because now I would be able to keep an eye on him and maybe start to put a dent in his steel armor.

CHAPTER SIX

Max

IT WAS JUST before nine in the morning when I pulled up out front of the address that Damien had texted to me.

I wasn't looking forward to spending the day with Damien. We had worked together in the past before, but that was different. We had been working a case for the Agency so there had been plenty of things for us to focus on. We had been chasing down a criminal. This time, though, there would be no suspects to chase down, no crime scene to investigate. We would be basically walking around checking out buildings and making sure Travis didn't get hurt in the process. There wouldn't be any buffer between us and I wasn't really in the mood to deal with him trying to judge or lecture me about my life choices.

There were only two reasons I was even here. First, I needed the paycheck. Second, and more importantly, it would allow me to see Travis. I didn't know him. I had only seen him in passing and I'd heard little things about him through the grapevine. What struck me the most was the fact that everyone had basically said the same thing. A nice, quiet, shy man who had a good heart. That wasn't the issue. It was all the things they hadn't said about him. There was never any talk about his personal details. Little details that usually came up in conversation with someone. No one knew where exactly he lived. No one had been over to his place. No one knew anything about his personal life outside of him being gay. He didn't appear to go out and hang out with friends or even colleagues at the end of the day. He kept to himself and where most people took it as him being shy and introverted, I couldn't help but wonder if something more was going on. To say the man and his possible secrets intrigued me was an understatement.

Lots of people who were introverted went out and got a job where they would have to deal with the public. I had seen it plenty of times and I knew when they got home at night they didn't want to do anything but crash on their couch and watch some television. All of that was normal, but Travis didn't come across as the type to me. I had a weird feeling it wasn't just that he didn't *want* to share personal details about his life, but rather it was almost as if he wasn't *allowed* to.

In the rare couple of times that I'd seen him interacting with someone, I would hang back and watch. Not in a creepy stalker way, but in a curious way. I wanted to see what I could gather from the man who had caught a lot of people's curiosity. Him not wanting to talk about anything personal had almost become a game with the people Travis worked with. As if they were collecting points every time they got a new piece of intel out of him.

Only, it seemed to me like it was a game everyone was going to lose, because Travis was extremely careful with his choice of words. He never let anything slip. It was as if his very life depended on it.

And that very realization was what made me so curious about him, because maybe his life literally did depend on him being quiet. He could have easily been on the run, but my gut said not from the cops, from someone dangerous.

Travis didn't come across as someone who had broken the law. He honestly came across more as a victim with his size and timid personality. He almost appeared scared of life, which was odd considering he wasn't that young. He was twenty-seven. He had enough years behind him to help teach him valuable lessons to make him tougher. Looking at him, I couldn't help but wonder what he might have gone through to make him that way. I was willing to bet his self-confidence was in the shithouse. That either came from a traumatizing childhood, shitty parents, or both. I wasn't sure just yet which category Travis fell under.

I wanted to know, though. The protective side of me was screaming out at me to protect him and try to make him feel safe. I didn't even know what I was supposed to be making him feel safe against, but maybe this was the opportunity that I needed to try and get some information out of him. To finally have a chance to sneak into his fortress and learn something that other people didn't already know about him. I almost felt obsessed with figuring the man out when no one else could.

I could also see the irony in the situation, because I was positive that Damien was trying to do the very same thing with me. Only, I didn't need anyone's protection. I was more than capable of taking care of myself and I didn't want or need anyone in my life.

I enjoyed being home alone. I enjoyed not having a connection to anyone who could either hurt me or leave me. I enjoyed having random one-night stands in the back of the clubs. Everything was simpler that way. Easier. No emotions were involved, no expectations or strings. Both parties knew it was just for sex and that names were irrelevant. Everything was simple and easy and I was not looking to have anyone come into my life and complicate things.

I saw both Damien and Travis pull up so I climbed out of my car. I glanced over and saw the both of them exiting their own vehicles and once again my gaze landed on Travis. He was wearing a long sleeved turtleneck and that instantly tossed up a red flag in my head. It wasn't that cold out. Both Damien and I were wearing t-shirts. There was no need for Travis to be wearing a long sleeved shirt, much less one with a turtleneck. That was overkill and I couldn't help but wonder why he was wearing one.

In the times that I had seen Travis, he was usually always wearing a long sleeve or a sweater or jacket. He never walked around in just a t-shirt, not even when it was a casual dress day for his job. I hadn't thought much of it before because

I didn't see him on a regular basis, but now I was starting to question it. It was just another piece to his puzzle and soon enough, I would have enough pieces to be able to figure out what the puzzle was.

"I don't believe we have been officially introduced. I'm Max Morris," I said to Travis as I held my hand out for him.

"Travis Manning," he said as he gently took my hand in his.

I ignored the light bolt of electricity that raced up my arm at the contact of his skin against mine. It wasn't that Travis wasn't my type, he was, it was that we were here for work. But maybe if I could get him to open up to me more, we could have some serious fun later on.

Travis quickly pulled his hand back and I couldn't help but wonder if maybe he felt the same electricity hitting him that I did. He scanned the area as he spoke.

"This is one of the houses we are considering using."

Both Damien and I turned to see the house that was across the street. The house was in rough shape, but I suspected that was by design. Social Services wanted to be able to renovate the older homes that the city owned to turn them into safe havens. It was on us to make sure it would be safe for the children who were seeking shelter. We walked inside and we all started to look around. It was in very rough shape, but it appeared to be all cosmetic work from what I could pick up.

"It's a low crime area," Damien commented.

"There's also not much around. That

could be a problem if the kids need help. There's no open businesses and the houses in the area are all rundown and either empty or homeless people live in them," I added.

"Which would be an issue if something happened. There wouldn't be any witnesses or someone who would call the police," Travis said with complete understanding.

When doing a threat assessment we had to focus on other factors than just the initial home. We had to focus on the other factors like who would potentially be around the children and who won't be. We didn't want the kids within the gang areas of the town because most of them needed safety. At the same time, we didn't want them almost isolated because if something did happen there was no one they could go to for help. We had to find a balance. It was why places like the suburbs were good for safe havens. There was safety within a community, even if the people around them didn't know they were helping to protect a child.

"I don't think this would be the best place for a safe haven. We need a more populated area," I said.

"I agree. We run the risk of having a nosy neighbor in a more populated area, but it would be better than not having anyone around. We also aren't that far away from the gang area. If they start to spread out into other territories, it would bring them too close to here," Damien added.

"Okay, then. I'll remove this place from the list of possibilities. Do you have a bit more time? There's another house we can check out.”

“We have all day,” Damien said, flashing a warm smile at me.

The asshole knew I didn’t really want to be doing this. Well, the joke was on him because I was very interested in spending more time with Travis. Even with us being inside the house, Travis didn’t seem to loosen up any. He still seemed like he was on edge, waiting for an attack to happen.

I was getting a bad feeling in the pit of my stomach. Whatever was making Travis this hyper vigilant and on edge all of the time, it had to be bad and I suspected it was still fresh within him. He had seemed antsy and anxious other times I’d seen him as well, but I had never seen it at this level. It could just be because he was in a new town and still trying to adjust to it, but I suspected something had happened to force the difference in him. Maybe even had a hand in him deciding to make the move down to Baton Rouge. Whatever was going on, I was going to find out. I was going to be keeping a very close eye on Travis and I wasn't going to stop until I finally had the whole puzzle completed.

And if he was in trouble, I would be there to make sure he was safe. If there was a threat out there looking to cause him harm, I would eliminate it. I wasn't going to allow anyone to hurt him, not while there was still breath in my body.

CHAPTER SEVEN

Travis

I SHOULDN'T BE here. I knew I shouldn't be here, but I felt like this was something I *needed* to do.

I wanted to wash away Baxter and everything that he put me through in order to start fresh. I needed a rebound, a one-night stand that meant nothing to me to cleanse my body and my mind from

Baxter. More importantly, I needed to remind myself what good sex felt like. I wanted to remind myself what an orgasm felt like. I needed this tonight, more than anything else. I had to be able to be myself. I had to be able to be out and proud again. I had to be able to have sex and enjoy it, to crave it like I used to do before Baxter came into my life. I needed to be able to feel free and that was what tonight was all about.

The club was packed and from what I had heard from the locals, this place was the number one spot in Baton Rouge for meaningless sex. It was also the hottest gay club in town and it showed. Even though it was only the beginning of the week, the place was full to capacity. Apparently, I wasn't the only one in need of a random hook up.

I made my way through the crowd to reach the bar. After ordering a drink, I took a moment to scope out the room. The club itself was actually pretty nice and well kept. There was a massive dance floor, unsurprisingly, that took up the majority of the room. Along the walls, though, there were booths that were lined red with a black table.

Even though it was a club, all of the dance floor lights made it possible for me to be able to see all around the room without someone hiding in the shadows. I really liked that. At least this way I would be able to see the people around me without having to try and guess what I was seeing.

The patrons were all very different from each other. I could see some clear manly gay men, the flamboyant gays, the cross dressers, the bears, and the spinners. There was a healthy mix in the crowd.

I myself preferred the manly gay type. I liked a man who worked with his hands, had muscles, wasn't too old, but old enough that games weren't involved. A man who didn't cling and could understand it was a one time deal.

That was supposed to be Baxter. When we met in that club, it was only supposed to be a one time deal. It wasn't supposed to go anywhere and that was something we'd both wanted. But then one time turned into two, and before I even knew it, he was practically living with me.

That wasn't going to happen tonight. I wasn't going to allow that to happen tonight or any other night. I wasn't going to be in a relationship for a very long time and I doubted I was ever going to allow another man to invade my home and live with me again. I had already done that and it turned out to be the worst few years of my life. I was determined that I wasn't going to be a victim ever again.

"Well now, isn't this a surprise," a voice said from behind me.

I knew that voice. I had only just met him earlier today, but I knew that voice. I turned to see Max standing behind me holding a drink in his hand. I had no idea he was even gay, so I was very shocked to see him there out of all places.

Most people saw me, they knew I was gay. It hadn't been anything that I kept hidden and my size didn't do me any favors. I was surprised that he was gay, though. I didn't expect that curveball.

I knew he had done some work for

Mason with the Agency and helped Damien out with his business. I never expected for him to be into men, though. I didn't get that vibe from him. My gaydar wasn't perfect, but it was pretty close. I knew Damien was gay from what I had heard and seeing him yesterday had only confirmed it. Max had slipped underneath my radar, though.

"I'm surprised to see you here," I said as he moved closer to stand beside me.

"In a gay club or a club in general?" he asked, flashing me a warm smirk.

"A gay club. I didn't know you were gay."

"I am and it's not something I hide, either. What about you?"

"Oh no, I'm out. I've been out practically my whole life." Not that my parents ever cared or noticed.

"Good, I never got the whole closet thing. People are happier when they are being their true self. People shouldn't have to feel like they need to hide a huge part of themselves from the world."

"I couldn't agree more," I said, flashing him a warm smile. It was refreshing to speak to someone who felt the same way that I did. I never saw the point in hiding that I was gay. It was a serious piece of me and I never felt like I should have to be ashamed of it or try and hide it away.

"So, what brings you here tonight? Looking for a boyfriend to kick off your new life?" he said, and then took a swig of his drink.

"No, not a boyfriend. Just looking for a quick rebound to cleanse my palette. You?" I didn't want to talk about Baxter. I didn't want to have to think about him.

Tonight was all about me and my own pleasure. Baxter had no place in my life anymore.

"Looking to scratch an itch. I've been pretty busy recently. If it's a rebound you are after, maybe we could help each other out," he said with a flirty smile and a wink that made heat wash over my body.

I would be crazy and blind to not notice how sexy Max was. He was exactly my type and under normal circumstances, I would have easily jumped at the opportunity to have sex with him. But we wouldn't be two strangers meeting in a club, and that posed a problem. I would have to see him tomorrow morning at work. I would end up seeing him around on different cases even once the current case he was helping me with was wrapped up. Hooking up with Max wouldn't be something that could stay here at the club. It would be reckless for me to sleep with him, so why wasn't I instantly saying no?

He held his hand out to me as he spoke. "Dance with me?"

It was a terrible idea and yet, I placed my hand in his and allowed him to guide me over to the dance floor. He turned me around so my back was pressed against his chest and his hands went to my hips, grasping me firmly. I couldn't help but tense up at his closeness. I knew I'd come here for some fun times, but now that I was going through with it, I couldn't help but be tense. Questions raced through my mind at warp speed.

What if it didn't feel good?

What if Max was just like Baxter and didn't even touch me?

What if he only cared about his own pleasure?

What if he didn't care that I didn't get off?

What if he was too rough or abusive?

I wanted to enjoy sex again. I wanted to embrace who I was, but now I was seriously starting to second-guess if this evening was even a good idea at all.

And what about my bruises?

There was a chance he would notice them. I was wearing a long sleeved shirt and I really only needed to drop my pants a bit, but if he wanted me fully naked, he was going to see the bruises.

Shit.

This was a mistake.

I shouldn't be here.

"Hey, relax. We're just dancing. Nothing has to happen tonight, we're just dancing and having a good time. Stop thinking, stop worrying, and just allow your body to feel," Max whispered, into my ear, his voice all sorts of growly and sending shivers down my spine.

I closed my eyes and tried to relax. Max was right, I just needed to relax and allow myself to feel good. I needed to stop thinking and worrying about what could happen. I could easily say no at any point, should I change my mind.

I felt Max gently move my hips in time to the bass of the music and I allowed myself to feel the beat. I swayed my hips along with Max as he pressed up against me. He felt amazing against my body and I couldn't help but wonder how incredible his skin would feel against mine.

As the songs changed, our movements got bolder. I started to get bolder. His hands against my hips started to trail up my torso and lightly ghost over the skin underneath my shirt. As his fingers touched my skin, they left a trail of electricity behind. I wanted him and I could feel he wanted me. His hardness felt very impressive pressed up against my ass and low back, and I wanted nothing more than to see it.

"We could go into the bathroom, if you want," he whispered into my ear.

I had never had a bathroom hookup before and it wasn't something I ever thought I would do, so all of this was new to me, but at that very moment it was the only thing I wanted. I had come here for this exact thing tonight and I would be a fool to turn it down. I could worry about the rest of it tomorrow.

"Lead the way," I said with a nod.

Max simply grabbed a hold of my hand and led me to the back of the club where the bathrooms were. I hadn't been here before, so I wasn't really certain what to expect. The second we walked into the bathroom, I noticed that it was empty, thankfully. I also noticed that it looked like a normal public washroom, only the bathroom stall doors had one hole in the middle of the door. It wasn't very big, but I was confused as to why it would be there. Max brought me over to the last stall and once inside, he closed and locked the door before his hungry mouth slanted over mine.

I instantly moaned at the sudden kiss and easily allowed Max to have full control over it. I didn't mind when the man that I was with took a bit of the control. I didn't need to be in control all of the time and I was good with letting the moment dictate who the aggressor was. I wasn't looking to be manhandled or dominated, I'd had enough of that from Baxter. I was looking for passion and someone who would show me pleasure to all new heights.

When the need for air became too great, Max pulled back a bit and spoke, his voice breathy as he panted. "Tell me you like to bottom."

"I only bottom." No truer words could have left my mouth. That was something I could confidently say and admit. I loved being gay and I loved to bottom. I held zero interest in even trying to top. When done right, the pleasure was indescribable being on the bottom.

"Fucking perfect."

I found myself being turned around

very quickly and I heard the sound of Max removing his belt. I moved my hands down to undo my own pants, not all that surprised that Max wanted to skip foreplay. I was good with that, because in the end, I just wanted to feel pleasure and come with a guy inside of me again. I didn't need to have any foreplay as long as Max could make me feel pleasure again.

Max placed his hands on my hips and I easily allowed him to move me into whatever position that he wanted. I spread my legs as best as I could to give Max proper access to my ass with my pants and boxers around my ankles. The next thing I felt was a cold and wet finger being pushed inside of me.

"Fuck, you're tight," Max moaned.

I knew that all too well. Baxter used to

tell me it all the time, but he had never bothered with stretching me before. It had been a long time since someone had stretched me first and the fact that Max cared enough to do it almost brought tears to my eyes. I had to blink a few times to fight them back. This wasn't about Baxter or any feeling associated with him. This was about me feeling good again and getting to feel true pleasure.

I started to moan as I felt Max add a second finger and start to scissor me, pressing against the tight ring of muscle to stretch me out. I was hoping that he wouldn't take too long, though. I needed his dick inside of me and I needed it now.

When I felt Max add a third finger and that finger hit my sweet spot, I couldn't hold back the loud moan that escaped my lips. It had been so long since I had felt that rush of pleasure and with just that one touch, I knew I had made the right choice by doing this tonight.

"I love that sound," Max said as he started to pick up the pace with his fingers.

"I'm ready, I want your dick," I moaned. I knew I wasn't fully stretched, but it was good enough. It wouldn't hurt anywhere near the amount I was used to.

"As you wish," Max said,

Max slipped his fingers out of me and I could hear him opening a condom and sliding it on. I couldn't wait until I could feel him inside of my needy hole. When I felt the tip of Max's dick against my pucker, I knew that Max was big; he was bigger than I imagined when we were dancing against each other.

Max kissed the back of my neck as we

both breathed heavily.

"This isn't going to be sweet and gentle," he warned.

"Good, I want it hard and deep," I said with a heavy breath. I didn't want it sweet and gentle right now. I wanted to be taken on a rollercoaster of pleasure.

I let out a deep moan as I felt his tip slip inside of me and I reveled in the burn as he stretched me even more. Max didn't disappoint. He didn't stop the forward motion, the intense pressure, until he was balls deep inside of me. I loved that he didn't stop or go slow. I loved that Max buried himself deep inside of me in one go. He knew what he wanted and he went for it.

Max didn't hold back after that. I felt him pull all the way out before he slammed right back in. I groaned at the slight shock of pain that raced up my spine, but I wasn't bothered by it, I knew it would turn into a deep pleasure soon enough.

Max's pace was hard and fast and the next time he slammed back into me, I felt nothing but pure pleasure. I had to fight to keep my moans from echoing off of the walls.

The sound of the door opening and footsteps told me that someone else was here, but it was only one person and not another couple. At the next powerful thrust, I had to bite my lip to keep the moan from coming out. I didn't mind someone else being in the bathroom, but I didn't exactly want to put on a show for them, either.

I felt Max's hot breath against my ear as he whispered, "Let it out. Let him hear how much you love having a dick pounding into your ass."

A sharp thrust from Max caused me to let out a very loud moan that anyone in the bathroom could easily hear. I figured there was no point in staying quiet now, the man obviously knew we were there and having sex.

Max continued to hammer deep into me and I wished that he would touch my aching dick. I would have loved to feel his rough hand clasped around my dick. If he didn't do it soon, I knew I would have to do it. I wanted to feel his skin on me, though, and not my own hand.

"Oh fuck," I moaned out on a strangled breath as a strong thrust just skimmed my sweet spot.

I heard the man's footsteps moving over to the bathroom stall and for a second, I felt a jolt of excitement shoot through my body. I had never had someone on the other side of the door standing there listening in before, I couldn't help but wonder if the man was jerking off at the sounds of our sex. There was a sudden knock at the door and I was not sure what the man wanted.

"He wants to suck your dick," Max whispered to me.

Those words caused my dick to pulse and some precum dripped out, sliding down to coat my balls. "I've never done that before," I admitted.

"Let him, it's exhilarating," Max growled into my ear as he guided me, pushing my hips closer to the door.

I'd just realized what the holes in the doors were for and the thought ricocheted through my mind.

They were glory holes.

I felt Max guiding my hips forward and when he put his hand on my dick, I couldn't help but whimper at the sensation. I allowed Max to guide my dick through the hole and a second later, I felt a man's tongue run along the tip of my dick. I couldn't help but moan at the contact of his hot tongue in my slit, his heated breath washing over my hardness. The fact that I had no idea who this man was only made the pleasure more intense. The man then sucked my tip into the heat of his mouth and I saw stars dance in front of my eyes. I had never been with more than one man at the same time before, and this experience was already blowing my mind.

Fuck," I mewled at the pleasure that was coursing through me as one man fucked me and the other sucked me.

"So fucking tight. Your ass feels amazing around my dick," Max said loud enough for everyone in the bathroom to hear him.

"Fuck, right there. Don't stop," I cried out when Max hit my prostate dead on. I gave up all hope of staying quiet at that moment. If either guy was bothered by my sounds, I didn't care. My whole body was singing with pleasure. Between Max's harsh thrusts hitting my sweet spot over and over again, and the mystery man's mouth, I was barely able to stand upright. My knees were weak, my legs shaky from the pleasure taking over my body. Not only was this mystery man incredible at giving head, he was able to take all of me in his mouth. I could not explain the amount of pleasure I was in every time the tip of my dick hit the back of this man's throat.

I was a moaning mess and as Max picked up his pace even faster, I knew I wasn't going to last much longer. After a few more thrusts, I felt my balls pull up tight and electricity raced up my spine as my orgasm hit. I let a loud and deep groan as my cock thickened and I came right down the mystery man's throat.

Max followed a few moments later and I moaned at feeling his dick pulse inside of me. I wished I could have felt Max's dick without the condom so I could have felt his hot cum searing my insides. I could feel each pulse of cum shooting out of him and my walls clamped around his girth with each one.

Once he stopped pulsing, Max pulled back, slipping from my ass, and I felt the loss of his dick inside of me instantly. The mouth on my cock had let go and I stood back up. As I started to get myself redressed, I realized the other man hadn't moved away from the door, and I couldn't help but wonder why. I assumed most would've walk away right when everyone finished.

My curiosity got the best of me, though. I had to know who had just given me quite possibly the best blowjob I had ever received before in my life. I reached out and unlocked the door and opened it. I couldn't believe who stood on the other side looking pleased with himself, and as the shock hit me, my jaw dropped open and heat climbed up my cheeks.

CHAPTER EIGHT

Damien

I HAD NO idea why I'd come to the club tonight. I had been so stressed and tense these past few months, I just needed something to take my mind off of it all. Something that would let me have some fun and forget about everything else that had been going on.

I had been to this club a few times

since I had been in Baton Rouge. It was a decent club and the guys here had a wide variety of types to choose from. I wasn't really picky. I liked guys that had some muscles, but I also liked the spinner type. I was more about personality than a set type. Tonight, though, no one was really catching my eye.

No one seemed to be interesting enough.

I had been hoping that I could find someone who would pique my interests. I was striking out, though, so I figured I would head out. I just needed to make a quick pit stop to the bathroom first.

I headed into the bathroom and saw that it was empty. The night was still young and I knew soon enough, there would be guys all over the place having sex and giving head wherever they could.

DAMIEN

As I stood there taking a leak, I heard quite possibly the most amazing sound I had ever heard. A guy was moaning from one of the stalls and I could hear the telltale sounds of sex coming from the cubicle. I had heard moaning before, but for some reason this guy's voice was sending shocks of electricity down my spine.

I had fully intended to ignore it, to just let the couple have their fun in peace, but I just couldn't seem to help my curiosity and excitement. Instead of leaving after tucking my half hard cock back into my pants and washing my hands, I stood there listening to the sounds coming from the two men in the stall. Just hearing the loud, pleasurable moans of the one man was enough to make me rock hard in a heartbeat, something that normally never happened.

I couldn't just stand here and listen to them. I turned and strode over to the bathroom door, flicking the lock, and then I went over to the last stall. I was about to do something I had never done before. I was going to suck a guy off when I had no idea who he was or what he even looked like. I had never utilized the glory holes in the bathroom at the club, but my body was screaming at me to do it.

I gave in to the demand.

I knocked on the door and I assumed both men on the other side knew what that meant. I had no idea if they would even be up for it. Some guys wanted to just get off in the stall and be left alone, while others were all too happy to have the added sensation of a third person from outside.

A second later, I was on my knees as a beautiful hard dick was pushed through the hole. It was thick and large, easily eight inches with precum already dripping off of its tip.

I ran my tongue along the tip, probing the slit and loving the flavor dribbling down the man's cock. The man let out a deep moan at the contact and it only turned me on even more, making my cock throb as it pressed against my zipper.

I sucked on the man's tip, and moaned in appreciation as another trickle of salty fluid flooded over my tongue. I could not believe how amazing this man tasted. He was sweet, like honey, and it was a new flavor for me. One I could get used to, I decided.

He was simply delicious.

I used my free hand and unzipped my

pants. Pulling my own rigid dick out, I started to stroke myself as I took as much of the man's dick as I could before my lips pressed against the edges of the hole in the door.

"Fuck," the man let out a throaty mewl, and I hummed around his length, pleasure coursing through me as I felt his cock twitch against the back of my throat.

"So fucking tight. Your ass feels amazing around my cock," the third man growled out and I could almost see his actions as he continued to pound even harder into the man whose cock was lodged deep in my throat.

"Fuck, right there. Don't stop," the man screamed in pleasure, his cock thickening as it slid in and out over my tongue.

They were no longer being quiet and I

was loving every moment of it. Their sounds were driving me insane and my own cock throbbed and twitched in my hand, precum leaking heavily from its tip. I had never been this turned on before and neither of them had even touched me. I was so close to coming, I couldn't believe it.

I could feel the man's dick getting harder and harder in my mouth as I sucked him deep again. He was so obviously close to falling over that edge, too. For the first time in my life, I wanted to taste this man's cum so badly. The need for it was so strong that I thought it would break me.

After a few more deep moans and erratic thrusts into my mouth as the other man obviously powered into him, the man was coming hard down my throat. I moaned as the taste of him flooded my mouth. It was the sweetest taste I had ever had in my entire life. The taste of this man on my tongue was enough to push me over the edge.

My balls pulled up tight and fire raced up my spine as I erupted over my fist with a deep moan, one that was followed by another long, low groan as the third man in the room came as well. I could feel myself pulsing as I shot rope after rope of thick, white cum onto the floor.

I sucked on the man's tip, making sure I lapped up every last drop of his sweet cum before I reluctantly removed my mouth from his still hard dick. I stood, tucking my deflating shaft back into my pants.

I knew I should technically be leaving; they were done and would be coming out soon. My part in this escapade was over and I should leave them to theirs. I knew that was the typical expected etiquette in these situations, but I couldn't help myself. I had to know who the other men were, especially the one that I had just sucked off. The one whose taste called to me on so many levels.

I decided the need to know who was on the other side of that door was too great and it was worth the risk of being told off by the obvious couple. Apparently, one of the men on the other side of the door was thinking the same thing, because I didn't even have to knock before it was quickly unlocked.

The door opened and there standing on the other side were two people I never expected to see. Max stood behind the man that I had just given head to and that man was none other than Travis Manning.

Both stood there with their pants still undone and their dicks tucked away. They were both just as shocked as I was, if Travis' jaw drop and Max's shocked expression were any indication. I couldn't say I'd ever expected to see either of them in a place like that, let alone on the other side of a bathroom door. I knew they were both gay, so the possibility was always there, I guess, but they never came across as the club going types.

I couldn't believe it was them standing there in front of me. That we had just done *that.* I should probably be freaking out and I was fairly confident that would come later when the high wore off from my orgasm. Instead, I simply flashed them a cocky grin.

"Imagine meeting you guys here," I quipped.

Max was the first to snap out of it. He reached over, with Travis still in front of him, and grabbed me by my shirt, pulling me toward him as he spoke.

"I wanna taste him."

That was all I needed to hear. I grabbed Max by the back of his neck and pulled him in for a kiss, pressing my tongue into his mouth. Max moaned at the taste of Travis on my tongue. Our kiss turned heated very quickly, both of us fighting for dominance that I eventually won.

Kissing Max was not something I ever thought I would be doing, but I liked.

I liked it a lot.

When the need to breathe became too much, I pulled back and then looked over at Travis. I could see the heat in his eyes. He was turned on by watching us kiss. I saw Travis' gaze travel down to my mouth and that was all I needed.

Throwing all logic out the window, I gently grabbed Travis by his jaw and pulled him in for a kiss. I quickly dominated the kiss, shoving my tongue into Travis' mouth. He moaned and quickly submitted to me, causing a hum of approval to escape my own mouth. Travis shivered, leaning into the kiss, and I could feel myself getting harder knowing that Travis was turned on by me, by us. By the time I pulled back, we were both breathing heavily.

"We should take this party somewhere more private," Max suggested, but he kept his gaze on me.

I had a feeling if I said no, they might

go off on their own and continue for another round. They were both still horny and Travis, he seemed hungry, very hungry. If I said yes, though, that could change everything. Right now, we were just three guys that hooked up in a bar unexpectedly. We could pass it off as an encounter in a dark club and call it a night.

We couldn't unring a bell, but we could ignore the chime.

The trick was, though, I didn't want to ignore it. As horny as they were, I was just as much. I wanted to feel their skin against mine. I wanted to keep kissing them and hearing their moans.

Just one taste wasn't enough.

"Where?" I finally asked.

"My place is ten minutes away," Max answered.

I glanced over at Travis and I could see he was all in for another round. Screw it. "Let's go."

Max and Travis quickly set their clothing to rights and once they were ready, we headed out. Max gave us both his address and we all climbed into our respective vehicles and made our way over to Max's place.

I still couldn't believe I was about to do this, but my whole body hummed with excitement. I had been with plenty of guys, but I had never done something like this before. I had never had a threesome and I was more than ready for it.

Could this be a colossal mistake?

Absolutely, but that was going to be tomorrow's problem. Tonight, I was going to have some fun.

***

DAMIEN

Once we arrived at Max's place, we were instantly heading inside and up to his bedroom. I was so distracted by them that I didn't even bother with looking around.

The second we were in his bedroom, Max was pulling Travis in for a heated kiss as they both worked on removing the other's clothing. I still couldn't believe I was about to do this, but at the same time, I was already through the looking glass.

I removed my clothes and made my way over to them. I placed a kiss to the back of Max's neck as my eyes landed on Travis, who was now naked.

"Whoa, hold up," I instantly said as my gaze scanned Travis' naked body.

Max pulled back from the kiss and I could tell he was a bit annoyed. That changed into anger as he saw why I'd said stop. Travis was covered in bruises, including one around his neck. They didn't look too old, a couple of weeks at most.

"Who did that to you?" Max asked with a deadly edge to his voice.

Travis simply rolled his eyes as he spoke. "It's from work. A father was upset that I was taking his son from him. His anger got the best of him, it's not a big deal."

"He choked you, that's a big deal," Max stated.

I had to agree with him on that one. The bruises weren't from an angry father who lost control for a minute. Nope. Not a chance. This was serious. The bruising around his neck was deep enough to tell me that whoever put it there, didn't let go until damage was caused. It wouldn't have surprised me if Travis had lost consciousness from it. I hadn't heard of a problem from one of the cases, but I would be asking Mason about it tomorrow.

"Okay, we could talk about past cases if you want. Or, we could do something else," Travis commented as he got down on his knees and ran his tongue over the tip of my dick, causing me to moan at the contact.

"We could do something else," I relented as I looked down and watched as he sucked my tip, his gaze meeting mine through his lashes. Travis let out a hum of appreciation as he took me all the way down to my base, something that wasn't an easy task. I was on the larger size and most of the guys I had been with could never deep throat me.

"Holy fuck, he can deep throat," Max moaned at the sight of it.

I threaded my hand into Travis' hair and pulled it a bit, causing him to whimper. Max came over to me and started to kiss me. As our tongues danced, I thrust my hips slightly, pushing myself even deeper in Travis' mouth. The sounds that were coming from Travis were driving me crazy and I knew that if he didn't stop soon, then I would be coming down his throat. Which would have been glorious, but I wanted to be coming with Travis' ass wrapped around my dick. Grasping his hair in my fist, I pulled Travis' head away from my dick as I broke the kiss with Max and spoke.

"Where's your stuff?"

Max just smirked as he went over to

his bedside drawer and grabbed what we needed.

"I want your ass up. I'm gonna pound into you while you suck his dick," I ordered Travis.

That sentence caused both Max and Travis to moan, Travis' eyes lighting with excitement. Max quickly grabbed the lube and a condom as Travis climbed up and onto the bed on his hands and knees. He spread his legs wide to give me proper access. Max placed the lube and condom on the bed, before he got on the bed to kneel in front of Travis.

"Wrap that pretty mouth of yours around my dick," Max ordered.

Travis hummed as he instantly took Max in his mouth. Watching them was driving me crazy and I knew if I didn't get to be inside of Travis soon, I was going to explode.

I smeared some lube onto two fingers before I slowly inserted them into Travis' ass. He let out a deep moan at the pleasure coursing through him as I made quick work of stretching him. I knew he had already had sex, so it was really just about adding some more lube so I wouldn't hurt him.

Once he was ready, I rolled the condom over my hardness and, without waiting a beat, pushed my tip inside of him. Even though he had been stretched a bit more, I couldn't believe how tight his ass was. It felt amazing as his muscles clamped around my dick. I pushed my dick all the way inside of his ass and once I was balls deep, I stopped, allowing him a moment to accommodate to the intrusion.

I couldn't believe how amazing this

felt. I had been with plenty of men in the past, but none had ever felt this good before. His ass was hugging my dick like a glove and I feared I could easily become addicted to the feeling. I glanced up and saw that Travis was devouring Max's dick like it was his last meal and I reveled in the sight.

"Fuck, those moans," Max groaned as he lightly shuttled his hips, his cock pressing into Travis' mouth.

I couldn't take it anymore. I pulled out almost all of the way before I slammed back in. I couldn't go slow even if I wanted to right at that moment. I couldn't believe how fucking amazing it felt to be inside of Travis as I watched him suck on Max. I never wanted it to stop. The intensity of the culmination of physical and visual stimuli was not something I had expected and it was driving me to the edge quickly.

Max reached over and placed his hand on the back of my neck, pulling me in to slant his lips over mine. I easily kissed him back, both of us fighting for dominance in the kiss and neither of us giving it up this time. The result was a very heated melding of mouths as our tongues fought with each other.

Max was the first one to pull back, he was breathing heavily and panting. I knew that meant he was going to come. Max's grip on the back of my neck tightened and he let loose a long, deep moan as his climax hit him.

"Fuck," Max moaned as his hips continued to twitch involuntarily and he emptied himself inside of Travis.

I pulled Max in for another kiss, one I quickly dominated as Max was distracted, still pulsing within Travis' mouth. I could feel myself getting closer to the edge, but I wanted to feel Travis come with my dick buried inside of him. I pulled back and spoke.

"Think we should let him come?"

"I think he's earned it," Max agreed as he pulled his semi-hard dick out of Travis' hungry mouth.

I used my right hand and grabbed Travis by the front of his neck in a very light touch. I didn't want to cause him any pain with the bruising already around his neck. I pulled him up so his back was against my chest, keeping my hand wrapped around his neck to hold him up against me.

Travis moaned at the new position and it made my dick pulse with need. I watched as Max got down onto the bed and ran his tongue over Travis' tip causing him to moan.

"Jesus, you taste so sweet," Max moaned, before he took Travis' tip into his mouth and sucked on it.

Travis moaned and I felt his left hand move over to my thigh, gripping it as the pleasure overtook his body.

I angled my hips and on the next thrust, I hit Travis right on his sweet spot. Travis let out a small scream and I could imagine the electricity the pleasure sent all up his spine.

"Fuck, oh fuck," Travis moaned as he moved his other hand up to my bicep, grasping it tight.

"You're so close. He wants to taste how sweet you are. Give him that sweet cum of yours. Come for us, Baby," I growled in his ear as I picked up my pace even more, hitting his sweet spot every time I pressed myself deep into his hungry hole.

I could feel the walls of Travis' ass tightening around my dick and I knew that he was about to come. In the next heartbeat, Travis let loose a deep, keening cry and then he was coming hard.

Max moaned as Travis' sweet tasting cum filled his mouth.

The tightness of Travis' ass clamped around my cock pushed me over the edge. I slammed into him as deep as I could and let out a deep groan as I shot my load into the condom.

I couldn't believe how hard I was coming. I had had mind-blowing sex many times before, and yet tonight had been even better than all of them combined. I couldn't believe how many times I was pulsing, still coming as Travis' ass kept a tight grip on my dick.

Max pulled his mouth off of Travis' dick and instantly moved to pull Travis in for a heated kiss. He shoved his tongue into Travis' mouth, sharing his own essence with him, causing them to both moan.

"See how sweet you taste?" I said into Travis' ear, causing him to shiver.

When Max pulled back, I used my hand that was still lightly around Travis' throat and I turned his head so I could claim his mouth for myself. I didn't think I would ever get tired of the taste of him. I felt Travis move his left hand up to the back of my neck as I deepened the kiss. I loved the faint taste of Travis' cum on his own tongue. He truly was sweet and I couldn't help but wonder what the hell he ate to get that sweet tasting.

When I finally pulled back, I removed my hand from his neck. Slowly, I pulled out of Travis' ass and got up so I could dispose of the condom.

Travis instantly collapsed down onto the bed as he breathed heavily. Max sat back on the bed and we both smirked at each other. We both knew it wouldn't be long before Travis was completely passed out.

CHAPTER NINE

Max

MY WHOLE BODY was tingling. I had had some pretty epic sex in my life, but I had never had sex that left me feeling this good. *Good* didn't even cut it; *amazing* didn't even cut it. I felt like I had just had the world's longest sex marathon and every inch of my body was feeling the pleasure from it. I had no idea sex could even feel this good.

People talked about threesomes all the time, but they never described it as that. They never said it could leave you ruined for regular sex. I had no idea that a case could turn out to be this interesting. I figured I would walk around the city with Travis and Damien and at the end of it, have a nice paycheck from it. I didn't think I would be having sex with them. Hell, I never would have thought I would ever have sex with Damien, of all people. Now technically, we didn't have sex with each other. We didn't even touch the other really. It was all about Travis.

Still, I couldn't help but wonder what his dick would feel like inside of me or down my throat. That man was very blessed in the manhood department. Typically, I was a top, but I had bottomed before. It was not something that I did often and I really had to trust the other person before I did it.

Damien had strolled out of the bedroom a few moments after we'd finished, to use my bathroom I figured. I looked over to see Travis completely passed out. I doubted he was going to be waking up any time soon. That was fine with me. I wasn't usually one for cuddling, but every now and then, I enjoyed not sleeping alone.

With the need for sex tamed, I could now focus on the bruising that seemed to cover Travis' body. I wasn't certain I believed him when he said they came from an upset parent. It was possible, sure, but I had a feeling it was something more.

Damien walked back into the room

and I could see his gaze instantly going to Travis' sleeping form. I had a feeling he also didn't believe the story. I got up and grabbed my boxers, slipping them on as I spoke.

"Beer?"

"Sure," he said, nodding as he grabbed his own boxers and slipped them up his hips.

I tossed a blanket over Travis so he wouldn't get cold before I strolled out of the bedroom. I made my way down to my kitchen and grabbed two beers from the fridge as Damien wandered out to my back deck. I stepped out onto the deck and breathed a contented sigh. The coolness of the night felt good against my heated skin.

When I decided to move down here, I had looked for a house that would suit my needs. I didn't care too much about what it looked like as long as it was in a good area of the city and had what I needed within walking distance. If I was going to live in a larger city, I wanted to be able to have what I needed within a reasonable distance. There was a cafe that served decent coffee just down on the corner. A Chinese restaurant and a pizza joint were on the opposite corner. There were three bars and a gym all within a block from me. I had neighbors, but they weren't too close. We didn't share a fence and I liked that.

The house itself had three bedrooms and two bathrooms. It was roughly eighteen hundred square feet. I didn't care about having a big house or what it looked like. This was the only house for sale in an area that matched my needs, so

I picked it up. It was an older home, but the bones were good. I figured I could always renovate it when the need or want hit me. I would rather use my money to take out my next target than to redo the kitchen, though.

I handed a beer over to Damien as I opened my bottle and leaned my arms against the railing of my deck.

"So, how's your night going?" I said with a smirk.

"Jesus," he said, before he took a drink. "This never happens again and we don't talk about it," he added once he swallowed.

"Don't worry, I won't tell your little brother about the threesome you just had."

"I don't have a brother," he said with an edge to his voice and I couldn't help but roll my eyes.

"You know, if you don't want people figuring out that you're both lying, you shouldn't be around intelligent people that investigate for a living. Neither one of you is fooling anyone. We know you are brothers. It's pretty obvious given how close you are. Not to mention you have similar facial characteristics. The question is, are you on the run because you *committed* a crime or because you *witnessed* a crime. I'm willing to bet it's the second one. Not because I don't think you're capable of killing someone, but more about those morals of yours. If you were a criminal mastermind on the run, then you wouldn't care about me killing pedophiles. But you do, because to you that's not justice, which tells me you are hiding from some criminal organization that you helped to get justice for."

He could tell people all he wanted that him and Sebastian were best friends, and I'm sure they were, but they were also brothers. There was no doubt in my mind that they were hiding because they'd witnessed a crime. And from what I knew of both of the brothers, they weren't the running away type. They were forced away because they'd testified.

I hadn't seen a US Marshal around them, so that likely meant they were completely on their own. Most likely the Marshal had been killed and they had to run. There was probably a leak within the Marshals and it would have been safer for them to go at it alone.

They were smart about not splitting up. Most would have assumed it would be better for them to go separate ways so they wouldn't stand out. The trick with that, though, was they would inevitably call each other or send emails and that could be easily traced. It would have been safer to stay together in the same town.

"I suspect that story that Travis told is a lie," he said, not even acknowledging what I had said.

I didn't know what I was expecting. I guess I wasn't really expecting for him to tell me the story, though. To trust me with that information. It would have been nice to have it, to know what had happened to them and how long they had been in hiding. To know if the threat was truly still active or not. He didn't trust me on that level and I doubted he ever would. Him and Sebastian had been doing this for a while. I was willing to bet they had been on their own for a few years at least.

I knew they had moved to Gaithersburg three years ago, so they had been in hiding for at least three years. He wasn't ready to let anyone else in and he had no reason to let me in. We didn't even really like each other.

"Of course it's a lie. He has bruises healing at different stages. He's anxious, always on edge, looking around, like he's waiting for someone to show up. He's been like that since the moment I met him. He's always wearing long sleeved shirts, sometimes turtlenecks. He doesn't release any personal information, doesn't let anyone over at his place," I listed off.

"He's being abused," Damien stated.

"Not anymore. His anxiety has picked up since I've known him. Whoever it was, he didn't move with him. And last night, he said he was looking for a rebound. He's trying to get over what happened."

It made sense why he was looking for a rebound. He had been abused and chances were his sex life had taken a dark turn and the common decency of mutual pleasure went out the window. Last night was about him taking his life back. It was about him having pleasure again and feeling like he mattered. He needed it more than Damien and me.

"Abusers don't always let their victim go," Damien stated and I knew that was all too true.

"Depends on how long they were together. Who his abuser was and if he is the letting go type."

There were two types of abusers. The first was the less dangerous kind, as hilarious as that sounded. They abused, but if their victim ran or left them, they wouldn't risk going to jail by stalking their ass and trying to kill them. They put their time and effort into finding a new victim instead.

The second type, though, were the dangerous ones, because they were the ones who didn't think they would ever go to jail. They were the ones that would stalk a victim across the county because the thrill of tormenting their victim was too great to turn away. They believed the victim belonged to them and they could do whatever they wanted with them. That the only freedom their victim would have is when they killed them. Whoever this man was that Travis had been dating, my gut said there was a fifty/fifty chance that he would follow him to Baton Rouge. And if that happened, if he got his hands on Travis again, Travis wouldn't be walking away. His abuser would kill him to make him pay for leaving in the first place.

"In my experience an abuser that chokes his victim that badly, they don't let them go."

"Personal or work experience?"

I highly doubted it would be personal, the man was huge, but he could have had a sister or his own mother could have been abused growing up.

"Work. I've never been abused," he gently answered.

"Loving parents,huh? What's that like?" I said sarcastically.

I had stopped playing the *what if* game a long time ago. The one where I created this whole world where I had two loving parents and my father didn't rape me for years. I'd lived within that world a lot growing up. I would tell myself that my mother was going to come in and rescue me from the life. And each day that it didn't happen, a small piece of me died until, eventually, there was nothing left. That's what people didn't understand. I'd died a long time ago.

"What about your mom? Where was she when you were growing up?" he asked, gently.

"Gone. She didn't want to be a mom. I found her six years ago, still working as a stripper and giving out blowjobs in the backroom for fifty bucks. My parents were never married. Phillip had been a regular customer at her strip club and one night she got knocked up. I guess I should be thankful that she stopped using cocaine when she discovered she was pregnant. So at least I wasn't born addicted to drugs."

"I'm sorry."

"Don't be. She was at least honest with herself. Too many parents who never should have been allowed to raise children, keep them because they think they have to. At least she knew she didn't want to have children and wasn't capable of being a parent. The best thing a shitty parent can do is step out of their child's life and let them be raised by someone who wants to be there. If Phillip had done the same, my life might have been completely different."

"Do you want kids?"

"Why, you want to adopt together?" I asked with a smirk.

"Some people like kids, some don't. I'm not burning to have a child, but I wouldn't say no if it was important to my partner."

I gave a shrug as I spoke. "I'm indifferent, I guess. Tomorrow should be interesting at work."

"We're three grown men, I'm sure we can be professional after a one-night stand. You good if I crash here?"

"You looking for round two?" I asked, flashing him a cocky grin as I looked at him.

He stepped closer to me, grasped my waist, and then turned me so my back pressed against the deck railing. He then placed a hand on either side of me, boxing me in before he spoke.

"There's that smirk. You're always smirking. I have yet to see a real smile on your face. You want to lecture me about being friends with intelligent investigators, but you have your own secrets. You see mine, but I see yours, too. I see your armor, the steel walls you have built up around yourself so you don't have to be hurt again. You never allow anyone to see any form of weakness. You never allow anyone to see your strength waiver. You're afraid to let anyone get close because you can't be hurt again like you have. You want to belong somewhere, but you're afraid people will see that you have demons. That it takes a lot for you to get through each day without the pain and sadness creeping in. You don't have to be afraid of me, Max."

My heart was hammering against my chest. No one had ever been able to read me like he had before and that scared the hell out of me. I didn't want anyone to get close. I'd built the walls up around me for a reason and I was not about to let anyone tear them down. Everyone was a threat and danger to me. The walls kept me safe. It kept people from getting too close, from seeing the pain that surrounded me all the time. I didn't want people to see the pain, to see that I was weak, because that was when they'd move in and take advantage of me. I was never going to be a victim again. I refused to be.

Before I had a chance to even form words, he leaned in and gently pressed his lips against mine. The kiss was brief and I barely had the time to respond before he was pulling back.

"See you in bed," he said, before he turned on his heel and headed back inside.

I needed to get my heart to stop racing. A single kiss shouldn't have me feeling this way, not when it was just a simple kiss. He was putting a dent in my armor and I wasn't sure how I felt about any of it. I needed to repair the dent and keep my distance from Damien. Starting tomorrow, things had to go back to being strictly professional between us.

Tomorrow.

I headed inside and made my way up to my bedroom. The second I walked through the doorway, I could see both Damien and Travis tucked snuggly under the covers in my bed. Thankfully, I had a queen size bed so we could all fit on it, barely. After turning off the lights, I made my way over to the left side of the bed and climbed under the blankets with my men.

Tomorrow.

I would repair the dent tomorrow.

CHAPTER TEN

Travis

THE FIRST THING I noticed when I woke up was that I felt warm and safe. It was an unusual feeling because I hadn't felt like that before in my life.

Ever.

I wasn't sure if that was more depressing or pathetic, but it was the truth. I had never felt safe before, not truly safe. I should have known what that felt like from growing up. I should have known what it felt like to be safe from my parents, but I didn't. Then the boyfriends that I had dated in the past never had me feeling that way, especially not Baxter. I wasn't sure why I had such bad luck with boyfriends. It was as if I had a sign on me that I couldn't find that screamed, *treat me like shit.* I really should stop dating. I should buy a cat and accept my fate.

I knew I wasn't much of a catch. I was thin, I bruised easily, and I was often tired no matter how much I slept. I also didn't know what real love felt like and I had never known real affection. I had a shit load of emotional baggage from my parents and past relationships. I wasn't exactly the type of person you lined up for just to be able to date. There was nothing special or memorable about me.

I slowly opened my eyes as I yawned and stretched. The first thing I noticed was that I was sandwiched in between two gorgeous men.

Damien and Max.

We were all in Max's bed.

We'd all slept in Max's bed together.

I don't know why, but it surprised me that we were still there. I knew I had fallen asleep, something that always happened with me after good sex. My body gets tired easily. It was why I couldn't work out or do anything too physical for long. I just didn't have the strength or the endurance, thanks to my protein deficiency. I would have figured Max would have woken me up to kick me out, though. I didn't expect for the both of them to curl up on either side of me.

We were all spooning each other. Damien was in front of me, with his back to me, while Max had his chest against my back. No wonder I'd woken to feeling like I was safely tucked into a cocoon. Technically, I was.

I would have loved to feel both of their arms around me while I was sleeping, but as it stood, they weren't touching me with the exception of their torsos. It would likely be easy for me to sneak out, assuming I could avoid waking up the two trained law enforcement investigators.

I was surprised to discover that I didn't want to leave. As a rule, I usually ran out the next morning after a one-night stand, but this morning I just wanted to close my eyes and go back to sleep cuddled up between these two hunky men.

To keep feeling safe and warm.

I knew I couldn't, though. This was a one-night stand. This was something that happened after a fun night out. This wasn't an actual relationship. No one was going to be making breakfast in the morning. We weren't going to be having a sexy shower together. We were just three guys who hooked up in the bathroom of a club.

The sex, though… oh god, the sex.

I'd wanted to feel pleasure again, I'd *needed* to, and they didn't disappoint. I had never felt that remarkable before in my life. I had no idea that my body was even capable of feeling that level of pleasure. It was the stuff that dreams were made of and I actually got to live it. I was actually able to have two guys pleasure me in earth shattering ways.

Just thinking about it was making my

body hungry for them. I wanted to feel the pleasure that they could bring to me. I wanted to watch as they made out and played with each other. I would have loved to feel both of them inside of me. I would have loved to watch as they went down on each other. There was so much I wanted to experience with them that we didn't get the chance to do last night.

Unfortunately for me, it would never get to happen.

This was a one time thing and that was something I was going to have to accept and move on from.

Letting out a soft sigh, I knew I needed to wiggle my way out of the bed and get out of there. We were supposed to have a professional relationship and now last night was going to make things awkward. As much as I would have loved to stay and see if any additional fun could be had this morning, I had to remember that we worked together. It couldn't happen again, because we needed to keep things professional.

I also wasn't ready to be in any type of a relationship. I had gotten out of an abusive relationship just two weeks ago. I still needed time for myself. Besides, they wouldn't want to be with me. Not only would it be weird to have a relationship with two guys, they wouldn't want to be with someone like me. I wasn't the picture of perfect health and I had too much baggage. I was too much work to be with. That was something I would need to accept for any relationship that I came across, even potential ones. Last night was just a one-night stand, and it was an evening that I would cherish for the rest of my life.

Very slowly, I started to maneuver out of the blanket and scramble off of the bed. I didn't want to wake them up. I didn't want the awkward *morning after* talk. I just wanted to slip away and do the walk of shame all on my own. I was relieved when Max just simply rolled onto his back, but he didn't wake up.

I quickly got dressed before I headed out. I wasn't able to lock the front door as I left, as it was a dead bolt, but the area wasn't dangerous so I figured it would be safe enough to leave it unlocked. It was also daylight, so the chances of someone trying to break in would be slim.

I trotted over to my car and quickly climbed into it. Only once I was in my car did I let out a breath I didn't even know I had been holding in.

DAMIEN

I was never really good at the morning after. It was why I tried my best to not have one. I always felt awkward and didn't know what I was supposed to do.

If I left and they didn't want me to leave, did that mean they would think I was a whore for fucking and going?

Would they think I didn't want anything to do with them?

Or would they be happy that I wasn't around because they didn't want anything more from me or they didn't enjoy the sex?

It was all very complicated and I never knew how to properly handle it. I turned my car on, shifted it into gear, and started to make the drive back to my place. I had work I needed to start and it would at least help to distract me.

***

The first thing I did when I got home was head into my bathroom for a shower. I didn't want to wash their scents off me, but I had to shower at some point.

I started the water before I removed my clothes. I didn't get in right away, though. I could feel the tingling all along my body and I knew what it wanted. Waking up with two guys around me had made me horny. I had two options, I could ignore it and focus on what I needed to do, or I could go into my bedroom and grab the sex toy and play with myself. Most of the time option one always won, but this morning my body was craving it too much.

"Screw it," I said as I pushed away from the sink and headed into my bedroom.

I grabbed the silicone dildo that I had, the only sex toy that I owned, and headed back into the bathroom. There was a suction cup on the bottom of it and once I got into the shower, I pressed it against the wall at the right height.

The hot water hit my body as I grabbed the body wash and added some onto the dildo. I turned around and bent forward, placing my foot up on the side of the tub and my hand on the wall right across from me.

Slowly, I pushed down and allowed the tip of the dildo to slip into my ass. I didn't stretch myself, but I wasn't that tight from having sex twice last night. I was instantly moaning as the dildo breached my hole. It wasn't a real dick, but it was close enough. At least for now.

I pushed back until it was all the way

inside of me before I started to move up and down it. A deep moan echoed in my bathroom as I hit my sweet spot dead on.

I wrapped my hand around my hard dick and started to lightly stroke myself. I didn't want it to be fast. I wanted to build it up until I couldn't handle it anymore and then let it all explode.

I closed my eyes and started to think about last night. I started to dream that it was Damien and Max inside of me. I allowed my mind to think about how good it would feel to suck both of their dicks. I imagined their hands all over my body. The way their mouths would feel wrapped around my dick. How amazing it would have felt this morning to wake up with one of them inside my ass and another in my mouth. The pleasure they would have brought me. I wanted to feel them deep inside of me. I wanted to feel their dicks down my throat, to feel them pulsing over my tongue and their hot cum shooting into me.

I wanted it all.

I let out a loud moan that I was certain my neighbors would be able to hear as I came hard. I stopped moaning as rope after rope of cum shot onto the shower floor where it was quickly washed away, swirling down the drain with the water.

I was breathing heavily by the time I stopped pulsing and I knew I was going to be tired once the pleasure wore off, but I didn't care. It was completely worth it. I looked down and saw that I was still hard; my body wanted more. I had no idea what was happening to me. It was like I was some horny teenager again. It was as if they had awoken something inside of me and the beast was starving. Insatiable.

I slowly moved my hand along my shaft and I hissed at how sensitive I was. It felt even better, though, and I knew this shower had just gotten a lot longer.

***

It was nearing three in the afternoon by the time I woke up. I had immediately gone to bed after my shower.

I had come four times before I was too exhausted to stand up anymore. It had been years since I had come that much and my body was not used to it.

I slowly rolled over onto my back and looked up at my ceiling. There was an old water stain on it and I worried that whenever it rained it would leak onto my bed. The problem was there was nowhere else in the room I could put my bed. The place I was renting was a very old and small apartment. It wasn't anything fancy, because I couldn't afford anything fancy.

I didn't make much as a Social Worker, but what I did earn Baxter had practically taken it all. He would run up charges on my credit card, and once he even took a loan out in my name. A loan that I was still paying off. Three quarters of my paycheck every month went to bills. It didn't leave me very much wiggle room for anything extra like groceries or a decent place to live.

Rent in Gaithersburg was a lot cheaper than it was here. Even in this one bedroom apartment I was paying twelve hundred in rent plus heat and electricity. And with me only making three grand a month, I was losing over half of it to my rent and utilities. Then I had a grand a month that I had to pay for the credit card and loan payments. Leaving me less than five hundred for my cell phone, a car payment, insurance and groceries. It was always tight and even right now I had no food. I only had twelve dollars in my bank account until next Friday. I was living off of canned food and frozen waffles.

It was part of the reason I was so thin. I couldn't afford proper food. Certainly not the meat that my body needed to help get protein into it. I was thinking I was going to need to look into getting a part-time job. Something I could do on evenings and weekends. It would be a lot of work I would have to balance, but it might be the only way I'd be able to pay all of my bills and be able to eat. It was something I was going to have to seriously start to figure out because I couldn't keep going this way. I was going to get sick and I was already at a high enough risk of illnesses, I didn't need to give my body any more reason to get sick.

Letting out a sigh, I reached over and grabbed my phone from the bedside table. I saw that I had a text message from an unknown number.

It wasn't uncommon for me to get a text message from a number I didn't have saved in my phone. Lots of people had my number. Different law enforcement officers, Social Workers, and even some of the children that I had on my caseload. They all had my number so they could reach out to me if they should need help. I opened the message and instantly my blood turned cold.

You think you can run from me? I'll be

seeing you real soon, whore.

He found me.

I don't know how, but Baxter had found me. I didn't think he ever would. I didn't think he would be trying to find me. I wasn't anything special to him. There was no reason for him to want to chase after me. He could have found someone else to have sex with. It wasn't like he loved me. I didn't think he would even try and find my new number. He never wanted anyone to know that we even knew each other. I couldn't imagine him trying to look me up or asking someone for my number. But he had obviously done something to find me. And he was pissed. I knew he would be mad when he discovered that I had left, but I foolishly believed he would find someone else to be with. I didn't think he would track me down.

I didn't know what to do. I couldn't change my number, that would look suspicious. I also couldn't up and move to a new town because I had a job here. I had responsibilities and cases I was working. I couldn't abandon these children that were in need. I had to be there for them, even if that meant I risked Baxter coming down here to see me. I just hoped that he was simply threatening me and he would get bored and leave me alone soon. It was a stark reminder, though, that I would never be free from him and I would never be safe.

CHAPTER ELEVEN

Damien

"WELL, WELL, WELL, look what the cat dragged in," Sebastian said the second I opened the front door.

We lived together, had been for the past fifteen years. We couldn't live alone just in case something happened and we needed to leave in a hurry. Living together for fifteen years had been difficult at times. There had been moments when having our separate places would have come in handy. It got hard to bring guys back to the house when your brother was sleeping in the room next to you.

Both of us were gay. It was weird how we ended up both being gay. One wouldn't think two brothers from the same parents would both end up being gay.

But as sure as the sun rises daily, we did.

Our parents were really good about it, though. Our father never made us feel like we were less of a man. He never gave us any shit about not wanting to be with a woman. He had even made sure that we brought our boyfriends home so he could meet them. Our mom, oh man, she was all for it. She never made a complaint about never getting grandchildren. Instead, she would go on and on about how we would be able to adopt a baby and that we could choose if we wanted a boy or a girl. She made us swear that we would give her one of each. Said for us to duke it out on who got the boy.

At the time, we both wanted to have children one day. Now, if we didn't get this organization eliminated, we would never have children. We couldn't bring them into this life. We couldn't risk their safety and welfare.

A child shouldn't have to fear going to bed at night. They shouldn't have to wonder what would happen when they woke up or if they would be woken up in the middle of the night and have to leave everything they owned behind. They shouldn't have to stop and think about what name they were supposed to give to someone, or having to leave school and their friends only to have to start all over again. It wasn't fair to them and neither one of us were going to be putting a child in that situation.

"You just been sitting there waiting for me to walk in?" I asked as I walked over to the coffee maker.

"No, but it *is* eleven in the morning and you are clearly doing the walk of shame," Sebastian said, flashing me a teasing smile.

I hadn't even woken up until thirty minutes ago. I still couldn't believe I slept that long. Normally, I'm up at six am regardless of when I fell asleep or what I was doing. Sleeping with Travis and Max had felt good, though, and I hadn't been in a hurry to get up and face the day.

At some point, Travis had left and I hadn't even noticed. I always woke up at the first sound or any movement and yet, I hadn't even noticed when the person sleeping next to me had gotten out of bed.

Very weird.

I didn't know what it was about either man, but when I was around them it made me feel lighter. Even as annoying as Max was. The whole situation was screwed up, because I shouldn't be feeling like this with both men. I should only be feeling like this with one of them. I was attracted to both of them, which was natural, but I wasn't more attracted to one over the other. I liked them both equally, which was surprising considering how often Max drove me insane. The whole situation was different and left me on uncertain ground. All I could do was wait and see how it would play out.

"There's no shame. It was a good night and I slept in. There's no mystery here, brother. What have you been up to?"

"Been helping out on a case for the Agency. Nothing crazy. I think Mason and Roland know that we're hiding something." Sebastian frowned.

"They know we're brothers and so does Max. They have all mentioned something to me."

"Shit, what the hell are we going to do?" He shook his head.

That was the question. We had never been in this position before. The people we were around had never discovered our secrets. Usually, our story of us being best friends worked without issue. People didn't need to look into it because we never let anyone get truly close enough to see through the carefully constructed illusion that we had to live with. Though, it wasn't all that surprising either, because normally, we only had acquaintances. We didn't have *friends* and we didn't associate with people in law enforcement.

Our business was typically kept small when we did private investigations. When we didn't, we were working on a ranch or for cash in a factory. We had decided to open our own business so we could have more steady cash and be able to take it anywhere we wanted.

Since being in Gaithersburg, though, we had been getting too close with law enforcement officials. At first, it was just Roland and then everything with the Agency started and now, federal agents and cops almost constantly surrounded us. It truly was only a matter of time before people started to figure it out.

Normally, when someone got close to discovering our truth we would pack up and leave, however, I wasn't certain that would be the right call to make this time.

All of the other times we'd been on our own. We hadn't had anyone that we could turn to for help or support. There had been no one who could help protect us, help us fight. That wasn't the case this time around, though, because we had an Agency filled with good men who would be there for us. Men who would help us fight against the organization and maybe, just maybe with their help we would be able to stop it once and for all. Leaving this time around, I didn't think it would be very smart and definitely not in our best interest.

It was time to stop running and fight back.

"We stay. We roll the dice and we stay. If they are able to find us, then maybe it's time we tell some people the truth. We're not working with factory workers or ranch hands this time around. The people we work with, the people that have become our friends, they are cops and feds. Men who can protect themselves and help us investigate. I think leaving this time around would be a huge mistake."

"We could be putting them at risk, though," Sebastian pointed out.

"Do you want to leave?" I asked, gently.

When it was time for us to leave, we always discussed it first. Unless we were attacked, then the choice was taken away from us. I never wanted to just tell

Sebastian what to do with his life or make decisions that affected his life without talking to him about it first. We weren't little kids, we were grown ass men who could make our own decisions.

I would never leave without him and I knew he would never leave without me. If we were going to pack up our lives and move to another town, then it needed to be a decision we both wanted.

I was hoping he didn't want to leave, because I wasn't ready for that yet. I enjoyed having our own company and working for the Federal Protection Agency. I adored helping children when they thought no one would be there to rescue them. I delighted in working with the guys and grabbing a beer with them some nights.

Most importantly, though, I didn't

want to leave Max and Travis. I wanted the chance to see what would happen next. Maybe we would go back to keeping everything professional and pretend like last night hadn't happened. But then, maybe something could also come from it. Maybe we could have an unorthodox relationship. I knew the chances of the three of us being together again were slim, but I wasn't ready to give up all hope just yet. If Sebastian wanted to leave then I would go with him, but it would hurt to leave this time.

"No, I don't. I like this town. I like the people. Hell, we have friends for the first time in what, fifteen years? I don't want to leave. I'm so sick and tired of having to start over, aren't you?" Sebastian asked and I could hear the exhaustion in his voice.

It wasn't an exhaustion that came from lack of sleep, but one that came from constantly having to be on point. We both always had to be vigil and on guard, always waiting and watching for an attack. It was exhausting on a mental level. After fifteen years of having to live that way, it was taking a toll on both of us and I knew if we didn't do something to change it, there was no telling what mistake we would make because we were too tired.

"Yeah, yeah, I am. I don't want to leave, either. I think it's time we take a stand. I don't know when the organization is going to come for us, but I don't want to run this time. I like the life that we have built for ourselves. I like our business, but I really like the good we are doing with our work for the Agency. I don't want to lose it, even if that means it could kill me in the end."

"Any job we take could kill us. We're not bookkeepers or bartenders, we help chase down dangerous criminals. At any given time we could be killed, what's one more possibility hanging over our head? If we were ever going to take a stand, this is the time we should do it. How do you want to handle it?" Sebastian asked.

"We can sit the three of them down and tell them our story. Have them over one night for a drink."

I knew it wouldn't be too hard to tell them what happened. They had already figured out that we were brothers so there wouldn't be any real shock. It was just a matter of finding the right time to tell them our story and who we were hiding from. I was glad that Sebastian wanted to tell them, that he wanted to fight. I didn't think I could handle running again. We weren't cowards. We didn't usually run from a fight, but for the past fifteen years that is all we had done where our personal situation was concerned. It was time that we took a stand and refused to change our lives once again because of those people. We had made a family here and it was time we trusted our family to be there for us and to help us end this war, once and for all.

Hopefully, when the battle did end, we would all be left standing. I didn't think I could handle losing any of them, especially Sebastian. Not after all of this time.

Not after fifteen years of fighting beside him.

It would already be weird if this did

end and we could have our own places again. We had been in each other's lives for so long that not having Sebastian there every morning would be hard. There would be an adjustment period for the both of us, but it would be a good adjustment period. It would be because we'd won and not because one of us was killed.

"They are on a case right now, but once it's done we can," Sebastian said.

"Sounds like a plan. I need to shower and then head into the office. What are you doing today?"

"I'm gonna head into the Agency and help out. We were working late on this case. Hopefully, Coop has been able to pull something out of his ass for us."

"The man has a gift," I easily said as I headed for the stairs. "See you later tonight. Be safe," I called out.

"Always," Sebastian called back.

We both had to be safe, but I knew he was protected with the guys from the Agency. Today, I had my own work I needed to finish up at the office and then maybe I would be able to relax a bit before tomorrow and the day started all over again.

CHAPTER TWELVE

Max

MY BACK SLAMMED into the wall as Damien's mouth devoured mine. Our tongues fought for control, for dominance, but this time I was not about to submit. I wanted the fight to keep going. I wanted to feel every ounce of passion that he had for me. I wanted to feel him against me, his skin against mine once again.

That one single time wasn't enough for me.

I was worried it would never be enough for me.

Ever since that night, I hadn't been able to stop thinking about either of them. We had been working together for the past week since we had our one-night stand and it had been torture on me. I was spending all day trying to control myself from jumping either one of them. Whenever I was around them, it felt like my skin was on fire. As if I had tiny bugs underneath my skin crawling all over me. The only time it got any better was when I was touching one of them. The closer to them I got, the stronger the urge to touch them became. I had never felt like this before. I never thought I would ever feel this way. Now that I did, I had no idea what I was supposed to do about it.

I let out a deep moan as I felt Damien's hard dick press up against mine. I *needed* to feel him against me. I needed to feel him inside of me. The need for it was stronger than anything I had ever felt before. Never had I wanted to feel someone inside of me this badly before and I didn't even care that we were in his office. That someone could walk in on us. We were alone in the whole building, but one of his guys could come in after wrapping up a case. I didn't care, though, I needed to feel him so bad it hurt.

Like an addict, this man was my next fix.

My fingers fumbling, I grasped on to the waist of his pants and undid his belt. Damien followed my lead and started to remove my own belt. We moved quickly, both of us being impatient. The need within the room was palpable. Neither one of us could wait much longer.

I kicked off my boots as my pants and boxers were pushed down. We were both already rock hard. I kicked one leg free of my jeans and Damien placed his hand on the back of my right thigh, pulling it around his hips. I moved my hips, grinding against his and rubbing our hard dicks against each other. We both gave a deep moan as the sensation sent a shockwave of pleasure down both of our bodies. Damien pulled away from the kiss and began to mouth his way down my neck, nipping, kissing, licking my skin and driving me wild with lust.

"Fuck, I need you inside me," I moaned out, as I arched my back trying to get more friction from him.

Damien let out a small growl as he ground his hardness against me. I could vaguely hear him rummaging through his pants and I really hoped he had lube in his pocket or something. The last thing I wanted to do was stop or settle for dry humming or a blow job.

I wanted him deep inside me.

Needed.

At the feel of his slicked up finger pushing inside of me, I let out the breath I hadn't realized I was holding. A whimper escaped my lips as I felt his finger going as deep as possible inside of me, pleasantly rewarding me with a faint brush stoke over my prostate. Just enough to tease and tempt, making me want more. Just one finger wasn't enough; it was nowhere near enough for me.

I continued to grind against him as Damien pressed open-mouthed kisses all over my neck before making his way back to my mouth.

Fuck, he tasted so good.

His special taste mixed with the salt of my skin left a heady mixture on my tongue. This time, I allowed him to dominate the kiss. I allowed him to have control, because everything was feeling way too damn good to try and fight against him.

He slipped in a second and a third finger, stretching my hole, and I knew I was going to lose my mind if he didn't put his dick inside of me soon.

"I need you. I'm good," I said as I pulled my lips from his, already breathing heavily. If he didn't fuck me soon, I was going to be coming and I wanted that to happen with him inside of me. I let out a small whine as he pulled his fingers out of me, already feeling bereft.

He searched around in his pockets again, but this time he pulled out a condom. He quickly slipped it down his length before both of his hands were on my ass and lifting me up.

I wrapped my legs around his hips and grabbed onto the mounts that were holding up the shelves he had along this wall. I felt his tip against my hole before he slowly pushed in. The second his tip breached me, I couldn't contain the loud moan that slipped from my lips. He felt glorious, fucking glorious inside of me and I knew it was only going to get better.

It was rare when I did this, when I had sex like this. I was usually the one who was on top and not on the bottom. There generally had to be a lot of trust involved and I had to be insanely attracted to the other guy for me to even consider bottoming. It took a lot for me to be able to have sex this way after growing up being repeatedly abused by my father. To push those memories down while it was happening, to combat the feeling of not being in control, it took so much goddamn energy and effort, and more often than not, it wasn't worth it. Sex was supposed to feel good and if I had to spend all of my energy on not remembering my past then it wasn't worth it.

But Damien, he felt amazing.

Every inch he pushed inside of me made my body feel like it was on fire. The only sound in his office was our heavy breaths as he bottomed out inside of me, his full balls pressed against my hole..

"So good, feels so good," I said softly.

"You're so tight and hot. Fuck, you feel amazing," Damien growled as he fought to not move, letting me accommodate the large intrusion pressed inside my walls.

"Move, I'm good." God, I needed him to move. I needed it more than anything else in this world.

He slowly pulled out before he pushed back in. He kept his pace slow and careful, allowing my body to adjust to his hefty size, and I appreciated him for that. The second the tip of his dick hit my sweet spot, I let out a loud moan and arched up.

"Faster," I moaned, needing more of him.

Damien didn't need to be told twice. He pulled out all of the way before he slammed right back into me, hitting my prostate dead on. I grunted, cursing loudly, not caring if people outside could hear me.

Damien's pace was brutal and it was exactly what I needed. I didn't need it slow and sweet; I needed it hard and fast. Damien's thrusts were so strong and my ass was banging the wall, sending some of the items from the shelves raining down to the floor. His hands on my hips grasped me so tightly I already knew come this evening there would be bruises there, but I didn't give a damn. My whole body was tingling and feeling amazing. This was the second best sex I had ever had. The first being the night when all three of us got to screw each other.

Damien either got tired of the position or sick of his shit falling all over the floor.

He held me even tighter in his grip, swinging around and bringing me over to his desk. I wrapped my arms around his neck as he bent forward and, with one swipe of his arm, knocked everything off from his desk down to the floor.

He lay me down on his desk and grabbed my legs behind my knees, pulling my legs up to press against his shoulders. The new position allowed him to go even deeper inside of me. His hands were once again back on my hips, pulling me to him as he pounded hard and fast inside of me.

I couldn't stop moaning and I was already feeling lightheaded from all of the panting I was doing. I could feel my orgasm building within my belly. I could feel the heat starting to spread, my balls pulling up tight against my body, and I knew it wasn't going to be long before I fell off that cliff. I was beyond excited for it, because I had never come without my dick being touched and I wanted to know what that would feel like. I needed to feel it just as badly as I needed to feel him throbbing and growing within me.

"Don't stop, I'm close," I moaned, arching back as he hit my sweet spot again.

"Come for me, Baby," Damien growled as his pace picked up even more.

After another three direct hits to my prostate, I couldn't hold off any longer. Black stars started to dance in front of my eyes as the heat completely engulfed my entire body and electricity raced up my spine. My scream echoed in the room as rope after rope of creamy white cum pumped all over my stomach. It felt like I was never going to stop, because each time Damien hit my sweet spot it would start all over again. I had never experienced this level of pleasure before in my life and I never wanted it to end.

Damien let out a deep groan as he snapped his hips forward, driving deeply inside my ass, and then I felt him pulsing inside of me as my walls clamped around his dick, and that only heightened my pleasure. He placed his forehead against mine as we both fought to control our breathing.

My whole body was tingling and I felt like I was floating. It was almost like an out of body experience. Like I could see what was happening, but my mind couldn't process any of it. I was up on cloud nine and I never wanted to come back down to Earth.

Damien lightly slanted his lips over

mine and we kissed, luxuriating in the intense feelings as our bodies calmed down from the high. I could have stayed here all day and night long. Hell, I could have gone another ten rounds with him if he wanted.

Sex with Damien was something I knew I would never get tired of or bored over.

All too soon, Damien was pulling back and he was slowly pulling out of me. I went to get up, but he placed his hand on my chest and looked right at me as he bent forward and ran his tongue along my stomach, licking up my cum. I moaned as I watched him.

It was sexy as fuck.

Once it was all cleaned up, he kissed his way up my chest over to my neck and then, he hovered over my lips as he spoke.

"You taste amazing."

"I know," I said with a smirk.

It did exactly what I was expecting it would. He crushed his lips against mine as his tongue invaded my mouth. He made sure I tasted myself on him and I had no problem whatsoever licking it off from his tongue. All too soon for my liking, he was pulling back from the kiss. Maybe it was a good thing that he did, because if we kept kissing there was no way I was going to allow him to leave this office until he fucked me again.

Damien stood up and pulled the condom off with a snap, tying the end and tossing it in the garbage can that sat beside his desk.

I let out a deep breath as I moved and stood up. My legs felt like rubber, my knees weak, but I managed to keep myself standing. It was going to take me some time before I would be able to get my legs working properly again. Not to mention my head was still feeling a bit lightheaded from all the lack of oxygen due to my panting in pleasure.

Shit, it wasn't even noon and this day was already out of this world.

"Sorry, you seem to have fucked my brains out, because now I can't remember what you were lecturing me on before you kissed me," I said as I traipsed over to where my pants were lying forgotten on the floor.

When I had come in this morning to see what the plan was for today, I certainly hadn't expected for any of that to happen. It had been a few days since our time with Travis and ever since, we'd all been professional with each other. We had never crossed any lines or even given any indication that something had happened. It was what needed to be done, but that didn't change that I wanted to be with them.

That I wanted to touch them and kiss them almost every moment of every day.

I seriously didn't know what had come over Damien. One minute he was lecturing me on where my dirty boots belonged, and the next we were making out. It was very romantic.

Hot.

"Dirty boots don't belong on furniture. I like to keep things clean," Damien said as we both pulled our clothing back on.

"Yeah, I can tell you like it really clean by the state of this office," I teased.

"This was all your fault. This mess

belongs completely to you.”

“Oh, it’s my fault? And how do you figure that?”

“You kept making sexy noises and driving me insane,” he pointed out as he started to pick his desk items up off the floor.

“I’m sorry, next time I won’t make any sounds,” I said as I held my hands up in a mock surrender.

Damien strode over to me and placed his hand firmly on the back of my neck as he spoke. “You better keep making those sounds.”

“I guess you’re gonna have to give me enough pleasure to be rewarded with sounds, then,” I countered with a smirk.

“That sounds like a challenge,” he said, before his lips were on me once again.

I melted against him, my body still filled with too much pleasure to do anything else. This man was like heroin and I was going to become addicted to him at this rate.

When the need for air became too much, we pulled back and I was already feeling the loss of him against me.

"So, now what? Was this like a one time thing or do we get to play again?" I asked.

I was really hoping he was going to say that we would get to keep playing. I wanted him so badly and I was worried he didn't want to keep doing this. I also couldn't help but think how it was a bit weird that Travis wasn't here with us. As satisfied as I was, and I was beyond satisfied, I was still missing the Travis's presence.

"I would like to keep going, if that is something you would be interested in."

"Definitely."

We both got dressed and I helped him to clean up the mess we had made. Thankfully, his laptop hadn't been on the desk but still in his drawer. There were a shit load of papers, though, and now they were all in a mixed up order and I knew he was going to be spending the afternoon getting it all back in proper order. The man did like order and I couldn't help but wonder if that was something that had always been a piece of his personality or if it was something new that crept up since whatever he was on the run from affected his life. Once we had everything cleaned up, I asked the question that had been burning my brain this whole time.

"Did you feel like there was something

missing when we were having sex?"

He looked at me like he was slightly confused and I could tell he didn't really understand what I was asking him, or why I was asking it.

"What are you talking about?"

"The sex was off the wall, don't get me wrong, but I kinda felt like we were missing Travis's presence with us."

Complete understanding crossed his face before he spoke. "I know what you mean. It's weird, because I enjoyed being with you, but I did find myself feeling like something was missing without him here. Maybe that's just because the first time we were all together."

"Maybe. I doubt he would be into a redo. He seems pretty adamant about keeping things professional. Not to mention whatever shit he has going on in his personal life."

We still hadn't been able to get anything out of Travis so far about his personal life. He was very good at not answering questions without making it seem like he was avoiding the questions. He had clearly been doing this a long time. Long enough for him to have mastered the art of deflection. He was also still jumpy and always seemed like he was waiting for someone to attack him.

We needed to talk to him soon. We had to help him figure this out, to work it out. We needed to make sure that he was safe and whoever was after him wouldn't be coming back for him. I wasn't about to let anyone hurt him. He was under my protection now, and I was going to make sure he was safe.

"We'll figure it out. We'll make sure he

knows he's safe and with a bit of luck, we can get him to talk to us. We have time."

Hopefully, we did have time, because if anyone tried to hurt Travis, I was going to kill them. For now, I would be keeping an eye on him and making sure no one was following him. I wasn't going to let anyone hurt him or Damien. They were my men, even if they didn't know it yet, and no one hurts anyone who belongs to me.

CHAPTER THIRTEEN

Travis

EXHAUSTED DIDN'T EVEN seem to cover how I felt. My whole body ached and I felt like my skin was crawling with ants. Nothing I did seemed to calm down my anxiety.

It had been a week since I'd received that text message from an unknown number, a number I was certain belonged to Baxter. For the past week, I had been plagued by endless phone calls at all hours of the day and night. Every time I answered, they would just hang up or breathe heavily on the phone. Whenever I ignored them, they would keep calling until I answered them. I wished it had been as simple as me changing my phone number, but it was connected to all of the children that I had on my roster, so I couldn't change it. And if I placed my phone on do not disturb, I could potentially miss an important or vital phone call from one of those children. I wasn't going to put their lives on the line because I wanted some peace and quiet.

It wasn't just the phone calls that had been keeping me awake, though, it was also the photos. The very next day after that first phone call, I received the first photo from Baxter. It was of me coming out of a potential safe haven with Damien and Max. It was one thing to be getting endless phone calls, but to receive photos of me clearly in Baton Rouge, that told me that Baxter was here and that thought was petrifying. It was either him or he'd hired someone to watch me.

I didn't think he'd hired someone, though.

Baxter didn't have money; at least, not enough to pay someone to follow me around. He spent most of his free time and money on online gambling websites, and he lost most of it. Whenever he lost too much, I had always been on the receiving end of things, which had been often. There was no way he was going to be able to afford to have someone following me.

Which meant he was here and he was watching me. He was biding his time and waiting for the right moment to strike. I knew he wouldn't do it right away. He was enjoying this game too much. He wanted me to be terrified and looking over my shoulder all day and night long. He wanted me exhausted and rundown so I would get sick and be even more vulnerable.

It wasn't good when I did get sick, because my immune system would become weaker from my protein deficiency. I had to be careful with getting sick. A simple cold could turn really bad and put me in the hospital, and that was the last place I wanted to be.

I was worried about Damien and Max as well. I didn't like that Baxter had been following me around, but I really didn't like that he was also following Damien and Max by association. They didn't deserve to be added into this drama and I hated that I was pulling them into it and they didn't even know it.

I knew they hadn't believed me when I'd said that a parent put these bruises on me. They weren't stupid, and I knew they wouldn't believe it, but it was better then the truth at that moment. I wasn't going to ruin the moment by telling them the truth. They wouldn't have wanted me and I'd needed to be with them that night.

I'd needed to feel pleasure again and that night had been remarkable. It had been everything I could have wanted and then some. The memories of it were still flooding my dreams when I did get to sleep. I'd swear when I woke up I could even smell them. I'd keep rolling over expecting for them to be on either side of me. And each morning I was greeted by disappointment when I realized that I was still alone.

Unlocking the door, I headed inside my apartment, coming to a dead stop as horror and fear instantly flooded my body. My whole living room area was trashed. My couch was cut up, deep slices marring the cushions that littered the room. Several photos that had been on the wall were shattered, their glass shimmering on the ground. The coffee table and the small bistro table I had in my makeshift dining room were completely broken, splintered wood everywhere. A quick look to my left showed me the kitchen had suffered the same treatment. There was glass all over the floor, as if someone had taken the time to smash every single dish I owned.

DAMIEN

The cupboard doors were hanging from their hinges, and some were also on the floor. All of my food had been emptied from my fridge and the condiments were spewed all over the floor and walls in a menagerie of colors. The fake hardwood floor that made up the flooring in my apartment had red paint all over it. As if someone had taken buckets of the shit and just tossed it all over the place. Some had even splattered onto the walls.

I was too afraid to look down the hallway to my right to see what the rest of my apartment looked like. I didn't need to wonder who had done this. I had been waiting for Baxter to come after me once I'd realized he was in town, and this was just him escalating.

He had obviously picked my lock, because I'd unlocked the door to get in.

He must have used his police lock pick gun to get in and out without anyone noticing. He'd wanted to send me a message that he could come into my home whenever he felt like it.

Message clearly received.

I pushed my door closed before I made my way down the hallway. The hallway looked about as well as I expected. There was more paint on the floor and the items on my walls were destroyed. The bathroom showed that the mirror had been smashed and my shampoo and body wash was squirted all over the place. I guess I should be thankful that he didn't break the tiles in my shower stall.

I headed into my bedroom, expecting to see the same treatment in the room as the rest of the house. Only, once again shock rocked through my core at what I saw.

Instead of it being destroyed like the rest of my house, it was clean.

There were fake rose petals all over the ground and in a heart on the bed. Candles had been set up all over the room, they weren't on thankfully, but the message was loud and clear. More often than not, if someone walked into their home and saw rose petals all over the ground and candles they would think it was sweet and romantic, but that wasn't what Baxter was telling me with his setup.

He was telling me how I was going to be his again.

How he was going to make sure he hurt me even deeper this time around.

There was a photo on the bed and I moved toward it with dread flooding my body. I expected to see another photo of me alone or with Damien and Max. I sure hadn't expected for it to be anything like what lay there among the petals.

It was of me, but he had photoshopped the image so I looked horribly beat up. The most disturbing part was the position he had placed me in. There was a thick chain, almost like one you would find on a tow truck, around my neck and I was hanging from the ceiling. I was clearly dead in the image and the sight of it turned my stomach.

Baxter was going to kill me and I suspected he planned to do it exactly how this photo was depicting. There would be no forgiveness this time. There would be nothing I could do or say to him when he found me to make up for running. He was too pissed off, too enraged for forgiveness.

He was going to kill me and there would be nothing I could do to stop him.

I had to leave. I had to get out of there. I couldn't stay in my apartment now. It wasn't safe. Before he knew where I lived I'd felt at home here, but now I knew he had found me and could easily get inside. I was no longer safe.

With shaky hands, I dropped the photo and raced over to my closet. I grabbed my suitcase and started to throw my clothes into it. I put everything that I could get to fit inside of it, leaving behind anything that wasn't important. I could always come back for the rest. Right now, I needed the things that I couldn't replace should I have to flee town.

With my suitcase packed, I fled out of my apartment, locking the door behind me, which seemed pointless given the state of the apartment.

I headed back out to my car, tossed my suitcase in the backseat, and scrambled into the driver's seat, turning the ignition before I'd even slid my belt on.

I rammed the shifter into gear, peeling out of the driveway, and started to drive down the road forcing myself to keep to a sedate speed despite the anxiety and high emotions flooding my system.

I didn't know exactly where I was going. I needed to find a hotel, a real hotel with a key card and someone sitting at a front desk all night long. If there was one thing that Baton Rouge had, it was hotels. I just needed to find one that would keep me safe until I could figure out what to do about Baxter.

The problem with that, though, was I

had no idea what to do about Baxter. I knew I could tell Damien or Max. Hell, I could tell the Agency and they would do something about it. But I wasn't ready to admit it out loud to anyone. I wasn't ready to reveal my shameful secret to anyone, but especially not Damien and Max.

I really didn't want to be seen as the domestic abuse victim that they had to treat like glass. I didn't want them to remember me as a victim or to remember me as the guy who was sick and tired a lot. I wanted them to remember me as the guy they had an epic threesome with. Someone who was fun and strong. Someone who they could remember without seeing all of the things that were wrong with me first.

No, I couldn't tell them, even if I really

wanted to be with them again. I wanted to fall asleep between them. I wanted to feel their hands on my body. I didn't want one more than the other, I wanted them both equally, which was exciting and terrifying all at the same time.

It couldn't happen, though, because I *was* the domestic abuse survivor. I *was* the guy who was thin and sick and tired most of the time. I wasn't the sexy, free spirited guy that they'd slept with. And if they knew the truth, they wouldn't want me. It was better to leave it to my fantasies, because that's all it would ever be.

That thought alone hurt so much more than everything Baxter had done to me.

CHAPTER FOURTEEN

Damien

I COULDN'T HELP but pace around our living room as I waited for the others to arrive. Today, we were going to be meeting with Mason, Roland, and Max to tell them our story.

I was nervous about that, not because I was worried they wouldn't believe us, but because it was going to bring more people into the situation. I didn't want anyone to get hurt, especially because of something that we had brought to them.

It was one thing to be hurt while on a case, but this was something completely different. This was a personal experience that Sebastian and I had gone through and it had nothing to do with a case that the Agency was working. We had made the decision to testify together. We had made the decision to go into Witness Protection. We had made the decision to keep going and live in hiding. They were all decisions that we had made ourselves and we had done it knowing full well that our lives were on the line.

What we were doing today, that was us bringing in people who weren't connected to the initial decision and that could get them hurt or killed.

"Relax, it'll be fine," Sebastian said as he sat down in the chair.

"Hopefully," I said, less sure about that fact.

"You're the one who suggested we stay here and bring them into the fold. That they already knew we were hiding something. This was your idea, so why are you having second thoughts now?" Sebastian asked, calmly.

"I'm not having second thoughts. I just don't like that they will be getting involved in it. The risk. I know it was my idea and I'm standing by it. They need to know if we are going to be around them and they already know we're not just best friends. The last thing we need is them looking into us and triggering a landmine they don't know they're supposed to avoid. I just hate that we are bringing them into it and it could get them hurt, that's all."

I really hated that Max was going to be involved in this. I didn't want him to get hurt. I didn't want anything bad to happen to him. I had no idea what was happening between us, but I was enjoying our time together. I knew we were just having fun. That we weren't anything serious. I doubted that he would want anything serious to happen between us.

Still, though, I was enjoying it and I was hoping that maybe we could have fun again with Travis. Being with Max those few times had been amazing, but I didn't feel complete like I had when Travis was with us. It felt like we were missing someone important and I was really hoping we could all enjoy each other once again.

It was a few minutes later when there

was a knock at my door. Letting out a soft breath, I made my way over to let the others in. I was really hoping this would go over well. I knew they had already figured out that we were brothers, that we were in hiding, but I wasn't certain they would be okay with what they were stepping into. Unfortunately, there was nothing I could do to take it back. Once they knew, they knew, and they would have to live with it.

"Hey, appreciate you coming," I said as I moved back to allow them to enter my home.

I could tell that they were already expecting what the meeting was going to be about. They had all been patient with both Sebastian and I. They had never pushed to learn more. They had never tried to get either of us to speak about what had happened in our past. I knew they had been itching to ask more questions, that they were curious to know what our story was and now, they were finally going to get answers. We all made our way over to the living room and took our seats.

"I'm not going to waste anyone's time by pretending like you three don't know that Sebastian and I have been keeping a secret. We are brothers and from New Jersey. For the past fifteen years, we have been in hiding; we've been running. Our father was an accountant for a major corporation. What we didn't know, was that one of those corporations was connected to an Italian mob boss named David Russo. There was some type of falling out between them and we witnessed Russo and his men kill both of our parents. They didn't know we were there; we hid upstairs until it got quiet. We called the police and we testified against him," I started.

"We didn't know that we would be in constant danger when we did. The police made it seem like we would be in witness protection with a Marshal until the trial. Then afterward, we would be safe to go back to our lives. Only when the trial was over, the threats kept coming in and we were told we could never go back to our lives. We were placed back in witness protection and five years in the Marshal who was watching us was killed. We suspected there was a mole within the Marshals, so we decided to go it alone. Moving all around the country, never staying in the same place for long. We managed. We didn't know that things would change when we hit Gaithersburg," Sebastian finished.

I could see in their eyes that they weren't surprised. They had already figured that something had happened to make us run. That someone was chasing us. I was happy and relieved to see that they weren't taken aback. I would have been more concerned if they were, because then it meant that they weren't certain *we* weren't the criminals in this story. It was good to know that they didn't think the worst of us. That they were truly on our side even when they hadn't known our side of the story.

"Is Russo still alive?" Roland asked.

"He is. We've been keeping track of him. He's almost seventy now, and we figured when he died they would leave us alone," I answered.

"We thought they would calm down after a while, but they kept chasing after us," Sebastian added.

"How do you know?" Max asked.

"There's been a few times when we've been able to get a head's up that they were on their way. We were able to get out. But there have also been times where they've gotten the jump on us. We've been keeping an eye on them and their movements, and so far we're still in the clear," I answered.

"How often do you usually move around?" Mason asked this time.

"Depends on the area and how active the organization is at the time. We've been able to stay in one spot for a couple of years and other times only a few weeks. Gaithersburg had been the longest so far. From what we have been able to gather, the organization doesn't know we're here in Baton Rouge, either," I answered.

"What do you want to do?" Mason asked the million dollar question.

I knew if we told them that we were already packed and ready to leave at a moment's notice, they would completely understand. They wouldn't pressure us to stay or try to change our minds. I also knew that if we told them that we weren't going to run any longer, they would step up to help us.

I knew it was my idea to tell them about it. That we had both agreed it would be better for them to know what was going on then for them to go poking around in the dark. Still, that didn't mean I was fully comfortable with them getting involved. With them potentially risking their lives for us. It wasn't their fight and they didn't deserve to be dragged into this mess. The trick was, we were already through the looking glass at this point.

"We've decided that we're done with running, no matter what happens. We wanted to let you know, because we didn't want to drag you into this mess unintentionally, and without you knowing the facts, the risks," I answered.

"We're not asking you guys to help kill them or anything like that. We just didn't want you to go digging one day and stumble across something that could get you hurt," Sebastian added.

"I can speak for all of us when I tell you that we're not going to sit around and let you both fight without backup. We knew someone was after you, just like we knew, eventually, there could come a day where you would need us. We're always going to be there for you both. Just like you both have always been there for us," Mason said.

It was a huge relief to know that we had their support. That we would be able to rely on them should shit turn up. Hearing them confirm it only made me feel so much better.

And I knew it made Sebastian feel better as well.

That didn't mean we were going to be stupid. We were going to keep being vigilant and making sure that our asses were covered. If an attack was going to happen, we would at least know about it beforehand and have backup. The whole thing had to end at some point, but I just wasn't sure when that would happen.

"We appreciate that," I said, flashing them all a warm smile.

"Do you have someone looking into their movements? Someone who can track them?" Max asked.

"We've been handling that ourselves. We didn't really know who we could trust and we didn't want to put anyone in danger," Sebastian answered.

"We can have Coop keep an eye on them, track their movements. We don't have to tell him what it's for. He'll do it as a personal favor to me, I'm sure. That okay with you both?" Mason asked.

I wasn't too sure how comfortable I was with that. I knew Cooper could sneak around online better than anyone. The man was gifted at hacking and computers. However, I also didn't want to put someone else's life on the line. It was bad enough we were already putting three others on the line and one of them was someone that I cared for.

Someone that I was sleeping with.

The last thing I wanted was for Max to get hurt because of me or something connected to my past. He was tough and could handle himself, I would never deny that, but I also knew underneath that tough exterior was a traumatized man. And the last thing he needed in his life was more pain. I looked over at my brother and he merely gave me a shrug, letting me know that it was my call to make.

Sebastian had always been easy going that way. He was always willing to allow me to take control and follow my lead. He used to do it when we were kids, back when everything was so much simpler. When this nightmare had first started, he often relied on me to make the decisions.

Especially, once the Marshal protecting us was killed.

It had suddenly all fallen onto my shoulders.

I was the one choosing the towns and deciding when we needed to leave. I was the one who came up with the rules, the most important being we didn't tell anyone. Followed by, we didn't allow ourselves to fall in love.

No relationships.

Sex was one thing, but we never brought them home. We never got attached and we never allowed them to get attached. At the time, that rule seemed so simple. Neither one of us could imagine that we would fall in love with someone. We both believed we were too broken for that. We had made peace with the fact that we would never have a family and a stable life.

Now, fifteen years later, that rule felt like a dead weight hanging over our heads. It was getting harder to push down the craving and need for love, long term companionship. One-night stands were no longer doing anything for either of us. I figured that Sebastian would be the first one to break the rule but now, it looked like I was going to be.

"As long as he's safe," I said.

"He knows how to cover his tracks. He'll be fine. Are you both going to be okay?" Roland asked with concern edging his voice.

"It's just another day," Sebastian said with a nonchalant shrug.

They all seemed to understand and it didn't take long before they were heading out. I walked them to the door but Max stayed behind with me on my front porch. I knew there was going to be a conversation about all of this. Whatever he had been expecting, I knew he hadn't been expecting it to involve the Italian Mob.

I went over to the far side away from the door and leaned against the railing with my forearms against it. Max mimicked my position.

"And here I thought I was the problem child," he lightly teased, and I couldn't help but chuckle at that.

"Oh no, you are definitely the problem child," I said, flashing him cocky grin.

"You gotta be getting tired by now. Running, always looking over your shoulder, that's a lot for someone to deal with," Max said with complete understanding to his voice.

"It wasn't easy at first. I was twenty, and Sebastian was only eighteen. His birthday had been just a couple of weeks before. I was in College studying business courses and he was all set to be taking the year off to travel around Europe. Life was so simple and then this shit happened and we were terrified. We had never been around violence before. Our parents were good people. We lived in the rich area and went to private schools. Everything was simple in life. We were terrified when we were first placed in WitSec and then, after a few years, that just became our life. It's funny, though, because after that first year there was a bit of excitement. There was something freeing about being someone completely different, moving around and starting fresh. We used to joke around about being spies."

Fuck, we were so stupid when we were younger. We had no idea just how dangerous all of that would be. Just how exhausting it would become. At first there was that bit of excitement and we tried to make the best out of the whole situation. That lasted until the Marshal was killed and we got another healthy dose of reality. We were bitch slapped by the reminder of the danger we were always going to be living in.

"I think it's natural that you would feel that way. When things get hard, your mind has to adapt and sometimes the best way to do that is by making up a different world. I used to tell myself that Phillip wasn't my real father. That he had kidnapped me, and my real father was going to storm through that door, kill him and save me any minute. I used to read different fiction books and pretend like I was living in them. I think it's how people's brains cope with the shit that happens to them. The shit that they aren't ready to process. Doesn't change that it's gotta be exhausting by now for you. It's been fifteen years. That's a long ass time to be on the run."

I couldn't imagine what he had gone through growing up. The world he had to have created just to be able to get through the day. I might have been living in a rough world, but he grew up in a cycle of Hell. A cycle I didn't think I would ever be able to survive.

"I'm so sorry for what you went through growing up. I couldn't imagine surviving like you have. I wouldn't have been able to do it. Look, you don't have to be involved in this. You've been through enough in your life, you don't need to take on my shit, too." I shook my head, waiting and expecting for him to agree he wasn't into that kind of life.

The very last thing I wanted was to get Max involved in any of this. I didn't want him to get hurt and I couldn't stand the thought of him being hurt because of me. He deserved to have a good life, one free from all of the pain and potential disaster.

"I'm not going anywhere. I'm already invested and I don't run away from something that is difficult or complicated. I like you, Damien. I'm here for you no matter what," he said, complete determination lacing his voice.

"I like you, too," I said warmly, my gaze meeting his.

He leaned in and placed a quick kiss

on my lips. I couldn't believe how good it felt to feel his lips on mine. I never thought I would feel this way about anyone and yet now, I felt this way about two men. It was insane, but I was tired of denying my feelings for both men. I was tired of not living my life because of fear.

The fear of the unknown.

The fear of being discovered one day.

The fear of losing someone.

I couldn't do that anymore, I had to start living so Sebastian would see that it was okay to start living. I had to do this for both of us, but especially for my little brother. After a moment, Max pulled back and I spoke.

"I don't want Travis to know. It's safer to keep him out of this."

"I agree. He has his own issues, and we still need to figure out what those issues are, too. My gut says he's not safe yet." Max stepped back but kept a hand on my waist.

I knew what he said to be the truth. Something was going on with Travis, and whoever was after him, I had a feeling he wasn't going to just let Travis go. We had to work on him and get him to open up to us. We needed to know who was after him so we could be prepared to stop him from hurting Travis again. It was something we were both determined to do.

"We'll keep working with him on it and make sure he knows he can trust us. We'll get it out of him and make sure he's safe. We won't let anything happen to him," I promised.

"I'm not going to let anything happen to either of you," Max promised, flashing me a warm smile.

Together we would make sure that Travis was safe and with a bit of luck, or rather a shit load of it, we would all be safe and maybe get the chance to be together.

I had no idea what a three-way relationship would look like, but I was willing to give it a chance if that meant that the three of us could be together and be happy. It was worth the risk and it would be worth the aggravation as we tried to navigate this new path in our lives.

We just needed to get Travis to trust us enough first and that was going to be a challenge.

CHAPTER FIFTEEN

Max

IT HAD BEEN three weeks since Travis, Damien, and I had begun working together on this large project. Three weeks since we had slept together. In the past three weeks Damien and I had slept together frequently, but each time it felt like something, *someone* was missing. Each time left me feeling incomplete with

Travis not there with us. It was insane, because we had only slept together that one time.

It shouldn't feel like that.

It shouldn't feel like I was cheating on Travis by sleeping with Damien. Something had to give. We had to do something because I wasn't certain how much longer either Damien or myself could last.

Travis had also been weird for weeks now. He was getting worse, more paranoid and anxious. Each day we saw him he was worse than the one before. I thought he would calm down once he got used to living here, but he hadn't. Typically, someone who had gotten away from someone who was abusing them they were anxious and worried for the first little bit, but as each day passed by without any incidents they grew more comfortable. It had been over a month since Travis had arrived in town and he should have started to relax a bit, but the opposite was happening. I was worried that something more was going on with him. That maybe he wasn't as safe as I had thought. That thought alone was enough to put me on edge. I didn't want anything to happen to either Travis or Damien, and I felt like I wasn't on top of things on either front. I didn't know what was going on with Travis and there was nothing I could do about Damien's situation. All we could do was wait and see if someone came for him. Not an ideal situation on any front.

I was trying not to let it change how I lived my life. I was trying not to let it taint our time together, but I was worried about

Damien being attacked and I wouldn't be there to protect him, either. I wouldn't be there to help keep him and his brother safe. I had never allowed myself to care for anyone that I had been with, and this was a good part of the reason. Even friends, I kept them at arm's length because I didn't want to have to bury someone that I cared for.

And yet, Damien and Travis seemed to be ruining me and my rules.

Coop was keeping an eye out on any possible actions by the Italian Mob, something I never thought we would need to do. When it came to the mob, the Italian one wasn't really that high on the danger list. Most of the time it was the Russians that you needed to worry about. However, the Italians were not afraid to get their hands dirty, as was evident with what had happened in Damien and Sebastian's lives.

Still, I figured after fifteen years someone other than Russo would be running things. Sure, when the boss ends up in jail they run it for a little while, but most of the time the vice president is jumping at the chance to run things on his own. They don't tend to keep playing second fiddle for this long. Russo must have something on his men that he is using against them to keep control of the organization. Maybe if we could figure out what that was, then they would leave Russo to rot in jail and we could get the target off of Damien and Sebastian's back.

All of that was going to take time, though, and I was going to have to accept that I wouldn't always be there for him in case he needed me. I was going to have to accept that Damien had been able to keep himself alive this long and that he knew what he was doing. At least this time around, he wasn't going to be doing it alone. He had the Agency standing behind him, too. If something did happen, we would be ready and hopefully, we would be able to end it once and for all.

Today, we were going to check out another potential location for the safe havens. We had been looking at a lot of properties, but we were trying to find the right options that would put the children in the safest home. The trick was we couldn't put a safe haven up in suburbia either, because then they would stand out too much, and just because they were rich people, that didn't mean they were good people. Some of the most dangerous criminals were white collar guys who knew how to fly completely under the radar.

We'd been checking out a lot of places, but only a few were viable because of the location and the people within the neighborhoods. We couldn't have the children around criminals because they could cash in on a serious payday. It was looking to be a longer process than we had expected for it to be.

I pulled up to the address and saw that Damien and Travis were already there waiting for me. We all got out of our cars and headed toward the house. This area wasn't the best, but I had seen worse. It was a solid middle ground and that was perfect for a safe haven. If we could make sure everyone in the area didn't have any criminal connections, this could be a viable option.

I kept my eyes on Travis and I could see him looking all around. His eyes were taking everything in and I could see he was scanning for any potential threats that could be hiding in the homes or around them. He reminded me of one of the Agents that I'd worked with who had to be medically discharged for PTSD. He was constantly on edge and wired so tightly that he couldn't even sit down. The hyper-vigilant attitude was a clear sign that something was bothering him and that he was expecting an immediate threat. Which told me that he had a reason to believe that his abuser was either here or watching him.

"Morning," Damien said to us.

"This the place?" I asked with a nod to the one house that Travis was parked in front of.

DAMIEN

The house looked rough, but every place we had seen was in rough shape, in one way or another. That's why the city was willing to give them to Social Services for free. It was going to take a good amount of money to repair the safe havens and I knew Travis had been working on some ideas to help raise the funds, because the city was only going to give them so much and it wouldn't be enough to repair the ten houses that they needed for the safe havens. The whole process was going to easily take a year by the time we secured the ten homes, generated the funds to repair them, made the repairs and found the adults to run the homes. It was a long process that we were just barely starting. Both Damien and I had offered to keep helping Travis with the process until it was complete, though. He shouldn't have to go through all of this on his own and we were not about to let him.

"Yes," Travis said as he unlocked the door and we made our way inside.

It looked just about as good as the other places and there really wasn't anything special about it. The houses themselves were pretty basic and simple to set up for security. Houses like these were all the same in terms of security, they had windows, and front and back doors to secure. Other than that we couldn't do much of anything for them. Anything drastic and it would call attention to the house and that was the very thing we were trying to avoid.

Damien and I went all over the house making any notes of anything that could be an issue, but nothing stood out. I headed back down to the living room and kept my gaze on Travis. I could see there was a slight tremble to his body. There were dark bags under his eyes; he clearly hadn't been sleeping. The tremble in his body could be from lack of sleep or from anxiety.

Either way, the shit had to stop.

Some people could handle being on the run and never knowing when an attack was going to happen, but most couldn't. Travis wasn't one of those people who could live their life never knowing if someone was going to attack him. His mind didn't work that way, and that wasn't a knock against him, most couldn't. The human brain wasn't designed to constantly be on high alert; it was why soldiers had so many issues. The brain needed the chance to relax and to no longer have to process every single thing they saw. That became impossible to do if someone was paranoid and on edge waiting for someone to jump out at you from behind a bush or when they were sleeping. Travis needed to talk to someone and I was done waiting for him to decide he was ready. It was time it got forced out of him.

"Okay, that's it, I'm done. We're all going to my place," I ordered.

"What?" Damien asked, confused.

"My place, now," I demanded, then I turned and headed out without further explanation.

I knew they would follow, Damien would be pissed about it, but he would follow. Travis would do it because he wouldn't know why I wanted to talk to him and he was more timid than either of us.

I knew I was supposed to wait until Travis felt comfortable enough to come to one of us, but that wasn't possible anymore. I wasn't going to sit around with my thumb up my ass just waiting for Travis to feel like he could talk to us when he was clearly risking his health. That had to stop. He needed help and he needed it now. He couldn't keep going on the way he was. With not sleeping and barely eating. Fuck, the man looked like he was going to disappear if he turned sideways. We had to do something and the option of waiting was now officially off the table.

As I made the drive to my house I saw their cars following me. I knew Travis was going to be a ball of nerves and Damien was going to be annoyed and pissed that I had given him an order like that, but he'd get over it.

The second I pulled into my driveway, I climbed out and strolled inside, leaving my door open for the others to follow me. I immediately headed over to my living room where we could sit and have this discussion, hopefully calmly. They both walked inside and Travis closed my front door as I spoke.

"Come sit down."

I took a seat on the couch and Travis sat next to me, but Damien went and plopped down in the chair so he could face the both of us. I could see the anger in his eyes; he wasn't happy about any of this, but he would be fine once I got Travis speaking. It needed to happen, Travis was getting worse and I couldn't stand around and wait for him to eventually trust us enough to open up, because he might never open up to us. He might never feel like we would care to know what had happened. Abuse victims didn't always talk about it. A lot of them kept their mouths shut for the rest of their life and suffered in silence. That wasn't something that I wanted for him. He deserved better and he didn't deserve to carry this with him for the rest of his life.

"What's going on, Sweetheart?" I asked Travis, gently.

I wanted him to know that I wasn't attacking him, that *we* weren't attacking him. That he could open up to us and we weren't going to lecture or judge him. A quick glance over at Damien and I could see that he now understood why I had us all come here. He leaned forward and did his best to relax his body and try to appear less intimidating, which was funny considering how big he was.

"Nothing," Travis instantly said, but it fell short of being convincing.

"We know something is going on. We know those bruises didn't come from a fight with an upset parent. We can help you, but we can't do that if we don't know what is going on, Sweetheart," I tried.

"Max is right, you gotta talk to us. We can help," Damien added.

"There's no fixing this," Travis whispered as the tears started to build in his eyes. His shoulders slumped.

Damien got up and moved so he was sitting next to Travis. I reached over and placed my hand on his thigh as I spoke. "There's always something that can be done to fix something. We can help, but you gotta tell us, Sweetheart."

"We know someone hurt you and we know that they were most likely someone you were dating. If he's reaching out to you, or harassing you, we can stop him. But we can't do anything until you tell us your story," Damien added.

I could see the conflict flickering through Travis' eyes. He *wanted* to tell us his story. He didn't want to have to carry this all on his own anymore and he shouldn't have to. He just needed to tell us and then we could help him carry the weight. Travis sniffed and a few tears started to track down his cheeks before he spoke.

"Joe Baxter."

"The asshole cop?" Damien asked, confused.

I didn't have any personal experience

with Detective Baxter, but I had heard enough from Damien, Roland, Jarod, and Mason. They had plenty of run-ins with him, and from what I had been told, Baxter was a piece of shit cop who was homophobic and had been Jarod's old partner that treated him like shit. He wasn't a good man and it was both surprising and not surprising that he was gay. It was a typical closeted move. Show off to the world that you hated gays and are a man's man, when behind closed doors you were either getting it up the ass or putting it up some guy's ass.

Also it wasn't surprising that he was violent. All of that self-hatred had to turn onto someone. He had to take it out on someone, because he couldn't take it out on himself. Travis was small, had a timid personality, and didn't have much self-confidence. It only made sense that Baxter would target him to be his secret lover.

"It started three years ago. We'd always kept it a secret because he didn't want anyone to know that he was gay. I thought it wouldn't last that long, that he would only want to keep things hidden until he was certain we were going to work out. But as time went on, he got worse. We would go on dates, but in different towns an hour away, and even then, he made it seem like we were just friends. When we were around each other at work or in town, he wouldn't talk to me or even look at me," Travis said in a shaky voice.

"When did it first turn violent?" I asked, gently.

"Not long after we started dating. I

dismissed it at first, believed him when he said he was sorry. I made excuses for it. He was stressed at work or he had been drinking, that I shouldn't have said what I said. Before I even knew what was happening, he was staying with me most nights and there wasn't a day that went by where I had a new bruise from him. Sometimes, it was from him beating me and other times him being too rough during sex. I thought maybe it would get better, that maybe he would accept who he was, but he just got more angry."

I could feel the fear radiating off of him and I hated that it was still fresh and raw within him. He was in a different town from that asshole and he was still scared of him. We needed to do something to help him, something to make him feel safe and not anxious and worried all of the time. He needed to start to heal from the trauma.

"He's the one that put those bruises on you," Damien gently stated.

Travis gave a shaky nod before he spoke. "He just got so angry. I was late getting home from work. He always expected to have dinner ready for when he got there. Isaiah needed to talk to me about the possibility of me moving out here. I wasn't going to take the job, but after Joe attacked me that night, I knew I couldn't stay. I avoided him for two weeks as much as I could and the night I left, I packed up everything and drove down here. I thought he would let me go."

"But he hasn't," I stated this time.

I'd suspected that Travis was getting worse and not better with the distance because whatever asshole he was running from had been reaching out. Turned out, I was right.

And of course Baxter was reaching out.

He wasn't just some random asshole, he was a fucking detective. If Travis told someone about the abuse, Baxter would lose everything. His career, his respect, his pension, plus if he went to jail as a cop, he would never get out alive. He needed Travis either terrified or dead.

"It started a few weeks ago. I got a text from an unknown number and it was him telling me that I couldn't run and he knew I was in Baton Rouge. Then the phone calls started to happen, just hang-ups or heavy breathing at all hours of the day and night. Then, I started to get photos of me and you guys leaving the different houses. Last night, I walked into my apartment and it was destroyed. There was a photo sitting on my bed. It was of me, but it was photoshopped. In the photo, I was badly beaten and hanging by a chain from some ceiling somewhere. It had a note written on the back about how he couldn't wait to spend the night with me. I packed up my stuff and went to a hotel."

"Jesus Christ," I said.

Baxter was in Baton Rouge and he wasn't going to leave until Travis was dead. He wasn't going to risk Travis talking to the police or the Agency. He wasn't going to risk his life and career. He needed to silence Travis for good and the only way to ensure that would be to kill him. If we didn't do something soon, Baxter was going to get his wish.

"I don't know what to do," Travis said

as the tears started to flow over his cheeks.

I instantly wrapped my arms around him and pulled him in for a hug. I saw Damien place one hand on Travis' back and the other on his knee. We were trying our best to offer him whatever comfort we could, but the only true comfort we could give him was Baxter dead. That was the only way Travis was going to be able to move on. I just hoped that Damien wouldn't fight me on it.

"It's going to be okay. We're going to protect you. He's never going to touch you again," Damien promised, a deep anger edging his voice.

Maybe I wouldn't have to fight him on it as much as I thought.

I placed a kiss on the side of Travis' head as we both continued to hold onto him and allow him to get the tears out. To cry out all of the pain and fear that he had been feeling and holding in for the past few years now. He needed this in order to start cleansing his body and soul from Baxter and the abuse.

After a moment, when his tears had quieted down, he pulled back slightly. I wiped the tears from his cheeks. I couldn't help but notice how beautiful he looked. His eyes, they were so expressive. I could see everything he was feeling. All of the pain, the fear, the vulnerability, it all lived and played out in his eyes. I hated seeing it. I wanted to see his eyes light up with joy, with pleasure. I wanted to see what he would look like when he was free from all of the pain. And I would see it, no matter what. I was going to make sure Baxter never caused him any problems ever again.

"You're gonna stay here with me until Baxter is dealt with and it's safe again," I said.

There was no way I was going to allow Travis to stay anywhere but here. He might feel safe in a hotel, but I knew from personal experience that anyone could walk through the front door and get someone's room number.

Shit, I'd killed ten people that way.

All Baxter would have to do is flash his badge and they would give him a goddamn room key. If Travis was here, then I would be able to have eyes on him at all times and know that he was safe.

"Are you sure? I don't want to put anyone at risk."

"I'm not going to have you un-secure in a hotel room. You'll be safer here than any hotel room. We can go and grab your stuff and check you out."

"Max is right. Baxter has a badge, it's child play for him to get into your room. You'll be safe here with us," Damien said and I was surprised by the *us* part of his comment.

"Us?" I asked.

"I'm not about to leave either one of you alone to deal with this. We deal with it together. We stay safe together," Damien said with a deep strength to his voice.

He was right, we were safer together, especially Travis. I had no problem with the three of us staying here, and I would be lying if I didn't admit that I wasn't half-hard at the thought of possibly getting to share my bed with both men once again.

CHAPTER SIXTEEN

Travis

I COULDN'T BELIEVE everything that was happening. I never thought I would tell anyone what had been going on. I wanted to deal with it on my own, but then Max and Damien had shown me the affection and care that I had been craving.

They wanted to keep me safe. They wanted to make it better and I couldn't keep it in any longer. I couldn't hold the secrets anymore. It was eating me up inside to keep everything to myself and deal with it all alone.

I had been barely sleeping and it had only gotten worse. I needed Baxter to leave me alone. I needed to feel safe and to finally get some real sleep. I was already constantly dealing with headaches and my entire body was sore from being so tense all day and night long.

They were offering me the chance to be safe and I had to take it. I had to get their help. It was the only way I was going to ever be able to be free from Baxter and start to heal from everything he had done to me.

Staying here with them both sounded like heaven to me and I was all too happy to spend more time with them. And I also knew they would keep me safe. Baxter wouldn't be dumb enough to attack me when I was around them. They were my guardians, my protectors, and I couldn't have been more thankful to them.

I could see the love that Max had within his eyes. He truly did care for me. Both of them did. It might be a mistake, it was going to potentially be messy, but I wanted to be with them. I wanted them both in my life and not just for sex. How it would work, I had no idea. I could barely handle a two person relationship, let alone a three-way relationship. I had no idea how that was even going to work, but I wanted to try and figure it out. Hopefully, they did as well.

But I didn't need to ask them about that tonight.

Tonight, I just wanted them close.

I looked at Max for a moment before I leaned in and captured his lips with mine. Max didn't even hesitate to kiss me back and he was instantly licking at my lips asking for permission to enter. I opened my mouth and welcomed his tongue, letting out a soft moan as his tongue touched mine.

Max placed his hand on the side of my face, cupping my cheek and running his thumb over my five o'clock shadow as he deepened the kiss.

I loved kissing, for some reason it was my favorite part. Baxter was never really into it, he said it was too immature. That there was no need to kiss when we could have sex. To me, though, I loved the intimacy involved with kissing. I loved how it made me feel closer to my partner.

It was one of the best parts and I never wanted it to end.

When the need for air became too much for the both of us, Max pulled back. I could see the heat and love in his eyes and I knew he was more than happy to continue this.

I turned to see Damien, who had been watching us. I could see the heat within his eyes, but I could also see the uncertainty in them. I could tell he wasn't sure if I wanted him there or not. He wasn't sure if he should be sitting there watching us or not. Traversing this relationship was all new to the three of us, but I wanted to make sure they both knew how important they were to me. How much I wanted them both.

Damien went to get off the couch, most likely thinking I wanted him to leave, but that was the last thing I wanted. I decided I needed to take a chance, so I reached over and placed my hand on the back of his neck before he stood up. I gently pulled him in for a kiss.

He easily took control of the kiss and I was once again moaning and whimpering as his tongue tangled with mine. I heard Max let out a deep moan as he watched us making out.

I felt Max's lips feathering all along my neck as Damien and I made out. Max leisurely trailed his hand down my chest to my pants. He easily undid the button and zipper, freeing my erection as Damien devoured my mouth. I groaned as Max's gripped my dick in his fist, rubbing his thumb up over the head to snag the slick pearl of precum that had gathered. I hummed into Damian's mouth as Max spread the moisture down my engorged shaft.

"That's it, Sweetheart, we have you," Max said. He nibbled on my ear lobe, then used the tip of his warm tongue to trace the shell of my ear, sending shivers skating down my spine.

My whole body was already tingling and we had barely done anything. I wanted them both so badly. No one had ever made me feel this good before and all I wanted was to spend the next week in bed with the both of them.

I let out a whine as they both pulled back almost in unison, but then Max placed one last kiss to my neck as he spoke.

"Get him in bed, I'll lock up," he instructed to Damien.

"You want to go to bed, Sweetheart?"

Damien, flashing me a warm smirk.

"Fuck yes." I wanted nothing more.

I felt Max stand and before I could even climb to my feet, Damien was scooping me up against the warmth of his massive chest. I wrapped my legs around his hips and started to kiss and suck on his neck as he took us upstairs. He got us to Max's bedroom and with the ease of him knowing the layout of Max's house, I instinctively knew he had been here since our one night stand together. The fact that him and Max had been together without me left me feeling sad. I felt like I had been left out. I didn't want to be left out. I wanted to be able to experience the pleasure with them. I was going to push that feeling away for tonight, but maybe tomorrow we would need to have an actual conversation about what was going on between the three of us.

Once we were in the room, Damien lowered me down. The second my feet touched the floor, we started to work on the other's clothing. Damien's mouth captured my own once our shirts had been removed. I moaned as I felt his tongue against mine as he fumbled with my button and zipper before he yanked down my pants and boxers. I was already hard and felt an overwhelming desperate need to feel them inside of me. Both of them.

"Fuck, you two are so sexy," Max said as he walked into the room.

Damien pulled back from the kiss and we both turned to look at Max and saw that he was removing his clothes, haphazardly tossing them to the floor in the corner. Once he was naked, he spoke as he joined us.

"How do you want to do this?"

"I want you both inside of me," I said.

I knew it would take more prep work, but they would both fit inside of me. I wanted to feel them both at the same time and not one after the other. I wanted to feel connected to them and for them to feel connected to each other.

I could see the heat in both of their eyes as my words sunk in. They were very interested and I knew this was something they hadn't done before. I got down onto my knees and took both of their hard dicks in my hands. I brought them closer together as I ran my tongue along both of their tips, causing them both to moan.

"Oh fuck," Max let the curse slip from his lips as I tongued his slit.

I looked up at them as I continued to

lick and suck at their tips. Damien pulled Max in for a rough and all consuming kiss. Seeing their tongues battling it out with each other only turned me on even more.

I wrapped my hand firmly around Max's long dick, pumping him as I took Damien's thick member into my mouth. I went back and forth between the two cocks, making sure to give them both equal time in my mouth. I had both of their combined tastes on my tongue and it was enough to make my own engorged dick throb. They tasted amazing, especially mixed together.

"Fuck, Sweetheart," Damien moaned.

I knew they were both enjoying getting to watch me suck them both off at the same time. They weren't the only ones loving it. I loved having them both at my mercy. I was able to give them pleasure and I knew they were in desperate need of coming.

"Your mouth feels so good," Max moaned. "Make us come, Sweetheart, then we can fuck you. Make you ours."

I let out a groan and then a whimper as I felt my dick swell even more at the idea. I wanted to feel them both inside of me at the same time and knowing that they both wanted it as well was only turning me on even more.

I took Max down to his base, his head hitting the back of my throat. Up and down, I sucked him harder and faster as his precum continued to trickle over my tongue. I continued to jerk Damien off at the same time, making them both pant heavily and hiss out noises that sent my senses reeling.

DAMIEN

I kept moving back and forth between the two of them. Taking turns to take one into my mouth for a few moments before moving to the other. Max was the first one to come deep inside of my mouth and I happily sucked and swallowed everything he had for me.

Once Max had finished providing his musky offering, I moved over and quickly took Damien into my mouth down to his base. I knew he was close and it didn't take long before he was letting a deep moan escape from his lips as he shot his essence down my throat next.

His climax complete and his balls emptied into my mouth, Damien pulled back. Cupping my cheek, he pulled me in for a deep, soul-consuming kiss. I moaned as I felt his tongue licking my own, sucking it, tasting the combination of himself and Max from my mouth

I could vaguely hear Max digging around in his drawer to find lube and most likely a condom, but I didn't want condoms. I wanted to feel them both inside of me. I wanted to feel the heat of their cum scorching my insides. Damien continued to kiss me as he lay me down onto the bed and I opened my legs as he fit himself between them. We continued to kiss for a moment before he finally broke the kiss.

"You sure?" he asked.

"Make me yours," I moaned, nodding. I wanted them so badly. Nothing else mattered more than feeling them inside of me at that very moment.

"We need to really stretch you to make sure you can take both of us deep inside of you," Damien said as he grabbed the lube and squeezed some out onto his fingers. "Turn over, it'll be easier with your sweet ass in the air."

I rolled over and shifted up onto my hands and knees. I lowered myself so my elbows were against the bed, making my ass stick out. I could feel Damien's index finger circling my puckered hole, getting it wet before he slowly pushed the digit inside of me. I relaxed with little difficulty; I knew it would feel good in a minute.

Max bent and took my dick onto his mouth, causing me to let out moan at the sudden pleasure that shot up my spine. Damien continued to finger fuck me with his index finger for a moment before he slowly added his next finger.

The pressure of his fingers made their way around the tight muscles, and the combined slurping and tugging on my dick by Max made my head swirl. I let out a grunt and then a whimper as Damien split his fingers wider inside me.

"I can't wait to get inside of you. I've been wanting to feel you wrapped around my dick again ever since that night. You are going to feel so good with both of our dicks inside of you, Sweetheart," Damien promised, his voice gravelly, as he started to truly stretch my ass and search for my sweet spot.

I moaned and gripped the bed sheets as the pleasure from both Damien and Max began to skyrocket. I arched my back and a long, profound groan bubbled from my lips as Damien's fingers hit my sweet spot and I saw stars. He made sure to continue to aim for the bundle of nerves as he added a third finger to my hole.

Max continued to work my dick with

his mouth, his tongue flicking repeatedly over that sensitive spot below the swollen head of my cock, causing my hips to jerk in response. He was unhurried, teasing me and trying to prolong my pleasure. It seemed like both of my boys were trying to milk me and it was driving me crazy, but the very last thing I wanted was for them to stop.

I felt Damien add a fourth finger so I could be properly stretched to be able to handle them both inside of me. I knew it was going to be painful at first, but I didn't care. The need to feel them both inside of me was too much.

Damien picked up his pace with his fingers, making sure to hit my sweet spot repeatedly each time. The feel of multiple fingers pressing against my prostate and the pleasure I was getting from the sweet heat of Max's mouth was driving me crazy. My legs were shaking and my hips bucked to and fro as my mind whirled, trying to keep up with the dual assault. They were keeping me right on the edge, but not allowing me to tumble off of it.

"He's ready, Baby," Damien said to Max.

It was that moment when Max stopped teasing me and gave the head of my dick a deep and hard suck as Damien rubbed his finger rapidly over my sweet spot. The combination of the two was exactly what I needed to fall off the cliff. I gave a small scream as I came hard and deep inside of Max's hot mouth. Feeling his throat constrict around me with each swallow only milked my dick for more cum. When I finally stopped pulsing, both Damien and Max pulled back, identical satisfied looks on their faces.

"How do we do this?" Max asked Damien.

"He'll be on his side. I'll face him and you will be behind him. I'll enter first as I'm bigger, and then you will." Damien turned to grab condoms and lube.

"I'm negative. We don't have to, but I'm negative." I let the words rush out as I moved so I was lying on my side like Damien wanted me to be.

"So am I," Max said, as he glanced at Damien.

"Me too. You both sure?" Damien asked.

"I am if you both are," Max agreed, nodding.

"Definitely. I want to feel you both." And there was nothing I wanted more than that right now.

Damien gave a nod and squirted some lube into his palm. He grasped his hardness and slicked himself up before he reached over and did the same to Max, who hissed at the pleasure. Damien laid down on his right side in front of me while Max climbed in behind me. Damien moved my legs so one was underneath him and the other fell over his hips so I was at the right angle for the both of them. Max began to trail open-mouthed, heated kisses all along the back and side of my neck as Damien spoke.

"You ready for us, Sweetheart?"

"Fuck yes," I agreed, nodding eagerly.

Damien lined himself up with my stretched hole and gradually pushed himself inside me, past the loosened ring of muscles. It wasn't too bad, because I had really been stretched out. He took it slow and I couldn't help but groan and pant at the pleasure of feeling his large size inside of me. Once he was all the way in, he gave a nod to Max so he could start to push himself inside of me as well.

"I'll go slow and if it hurts too much just say stop," Max said as he notched his tip against my hole beside Damien's cock.

"Okay," I panted, anticipation turning my mind to mush at that moment and making any other words impossible. I turned my head and started to kiss him to reassure him that I was all right with it.

He slowly started to push himself inside of me as he gently kissed me back. It was tight, it was really tight now, but Max had been able to press his tip inside of me and that instantly had the three of us groaning.

I broke from the kiss as I couldn't help but pant harder as Max slowly pushed himself inside of me, inch by glorious burning inch, stretching my hole beyond my imagination. He went slow, but he didn't stop until his hips pressed against my back and he was completely buried inside of me. I felt like any more than that and they'd split me in two.

I alternated between hissing out my breath and sucking another in as they both paused for a moment and my hole accommodated both men. By the time they were both balls deep inside of my ass, we were all panting and trembling with the need. It was more than just a need for pleasure, though. I could see it in both of their eyes. They felt that connection just like I did. As if our souls were connecting with each other for the very first time. The power of it was exhilarating and almost strong enough to make me come.

"Holy shit. So tight," Damien moaned as he licked at the sweat trickling along my neck. I moaned and threw my head back to give him even better access.

"Let us know when you are ready for us to move," Max said, clearly not wanting to rush anything, but I could hear in the quiver of his voice how desperate he was for me to give them the go ahead.

"I'm good move. Please, move," I begged.

I needed to feel them inside of me as they chased their pleasure. I needed to feel them pulsing within me more than anything I had ever needed in my life. I felt like I needed it more at that moment than I needed oxygen.

Max was the first one to gradually start to pull himself out. Once he was almost all of the way out, Damien began to slowly move in the opposite direction as Max pushed back inside of me. It took them a few tries to get the right timing down, but soon they had it so that one of them was pushing inside of me at all times. They were both aiming for my sweet spot and managed to hit it each time dead on, amping up my pleasure to extreme proportions. I couldn't stop moaning. My whole body felt like it was on fire and they were gasoline. With each thrust my body was getting hotter and hotter. The pleasure was on a whole new level, a level I didn't even realize was possible to achieve. The last time we had sex together it had been earth shattering, but this, I didn't even know how to describe it. There were no words to the level of pleasure that these men were bringing to me. I had never felt anything so incredible in all my life.

"Shit, this feels so good," Damien moaned as he picked up his pace, which only encouraged Max to do the same.

"So tight. So fucking hot," Max moaned, punching his hips even faster.

The pace of both men pounding into me was brutal and I was loving every second of it. I couldn't even form words, all I could do was moan and pant as the pleasure filled every cell in my body. With their brutal pace and the constant pleasurable assault on my sweet spot, I was soon seeing stars and coming with a loud scream. My whole body went rigid and I arched my back as rope after rope of hot cum shot out of my dick to coat over my belly and Damien's.

"Oh fuck," Max yelled. They both moaned as the tightness of my ass squeezed both of their dicks even more.

"Shit," Damien hissed, his fingers gripping my hips as he thrust deep inside me once more. I knew I would have bruises tomorrow but at that moment I didn't care.

I had no idea who came first, but I let out a deep moan and pulsed even more as I felt both their searing cum soaking my insides. Words could not describe how remarkable it felt to feel their combined liquid inside of me. To feel it painting my walls and knowing that I had been marked by both of them.

I belonged to them.

We all belonged to each other.

The room was filled with our heavy

breathing as we all tried to calm our bodies down from the great high. My whole body tingled from the pleasure and lack of oxygen from panting so badly. I didn't care, though, because it had been more than worth it. And that was the last thought on my mind before everything went dark as sleep overtook me.

CHAPTER SEVENTEEN

Damien

MAX LET OUT a deep moan, a verbal indication of the pleasure that shot through him at that moment, that turned me on even more. He was currently buried deep inside of Travis' ass while I was buried deep inside of him. When the three of us woke up this morning, we were all hard and horny, and figured a sex train was the best way for the three of us to be pleasured. We were all perched on our knees on the bed with Travis in front, followed by Max, and then myself.

It was interesting, though, because Max truly held most of the power and control for all of our pleasure. He had to be the one to move so he could pound into Travis, but as he moved back, he ground himself onto my own dick. The position was not something I ever thought I would be doing, but I was enjoying it a great deal. The physical feelings and pleasure combined with the visual aspect was a new sensation indeed and one I would happily participate in again.

"Oh don't stop. I'm so close, Baby," Travis whimpered, shifting his hips backward.

I reached around to grasp his dick in

my fist and started to jerk him off as Max continued his brutal pace, shuttling into Travis' hole. The second my hand touched his rock hard dick, Travis let out a keening cry and I could tell he was going to be flying off of the cliff soon enough.

"You both are so fucking sexy," I said as I pressed my lips along the back of Max's neck, causing him to moan and shift his hips as he powered into Travis and then back onto my cock even harder. Travis' cock swelled in my hand, Max's ass clamped hard around my girth, and my balls pulled up tight. I knew at that moment none of us would last much longer.

I never thought sex could ever feel this amazing. I had never been one for sleeping next to someone before, but waking up this morning with both of my men in my bed, it felt beyond wonderful. Even now, I was getting to pleasure both of my boys at the same time and it was only heightening my own pleasure.

Travis was a moaning mess and we both knew he was just about to come. I picked up my pace as I moved my hand up and down his shaft and after a hard thrust from Max, Travis let out a scream as he came into my fist.

I felt his cum covering my hand and once he finished pulsing, I removed my hand from his length and instantly brought it up to Max's mouth. Max flicked out his tongue and started to lick up Travis' cum without any hesitation. I knew he loved the taste of our sweet boy and I could relate to the enjoyment he was getting out of the action.

Once my hand was clean, I placed both

of my hands on Travis' hips and held him in place.

"My turn to be in control," I growled into Max's ear and it made his body shiver.

I pulled myself out almost all of the way before I slammed right back into Max, causing him to grunt as my dick hit his sweet spot dead on. It also pushed his hard dick deeper inside of Travis' sensitive body. Max made sure he stayed where he was, balls deep in Travis as I started to pound into him at a fast and brutal pace.

We were both on that edge, ready to come, and I was going to be making sure he reached his peak first. With each thrust, I made sure to hit Max's sweet spot dead on, relishing the grunts and groans I drew from his body with each fevered thrust. Both Max and Travis couldn't stop moaning and groaning as the pleasure within their bodies took over and the sounds both thrilled me and pushed me closer to my own climax.

"You feel so good, Baby. So tight, so hot," I moaned as I shuttled my hips even faster and harder. I was so close, but I wanted Max to come first. I wanted to feel the tightening of his walls as he clamped down around my dick. I *needed* to feel his ass milking me for everything that I had to offer.

"You want him to fill you up, Sweetheart?" I said to Travis.

Travis let out a profound groan before he was able to form any words. "Fuck yes. I want to feel it. Come for us, Baby. Fill my ass with your hot jizz."

I pounded Max's prostate a few more

times before he finally let out a long, throaty moan as he came hard and deep inside of Travis. The pleasure from it caused Travis to moan, too, and I knew he was coming once again.

I had managed to milk both of my boys and that pleasure alone was enough to push me over the edge. I snapped my hips forward and kept my dick buried as deep as I could inside of Max's ass as I pulsed and released every drop of cum that I had for him, coating his inner walls with pulse after pulse as my dick throbbed. I knew all of our bodies were screaming out in pleasure in unison and the thought made my head spin.

Once we all finished our respective climaxes while we each held tight to the man in front of us, we all collapsed down onto the bed. We were all breathing heavily and I knew we were going to need a minute before any of our legs would start to work once again. If this was what it was going to be like in the morning waking up to my men, then I never wanted to leave the house. I wanted to keep them both hostage so we could continue to enjoy ourselves in the same way every single morning—what an incredible way to start the day—and all day long for that matter.

"I think we broke him," Max said with a smirk as Travis swiftly fell back to sleep.

Max may have been right about that, but I could admit that these two might also break me if we started every morning like that. The first time we all had sex, I could chalk that up to being an exciting time with my first threesome. It only made sense that the sex would be off the wall amazing. But now, after three times, I still felt like my whole world had been shattered. Everything I knew about myself and expected for my future had changed in the space of a couple of weeks and the thought left me mind blown.

I never thought I would be in this position. I never thought I would be in a relationship, even just a sexual one, with two other men. It was insane and I honestly had no idea how well this was going to end or what would happen, but I wasn't going to allow fear of the future to dictate what happened between us. I wasn't going to allow that uncertainty to control what I did. I was having fun. I was finally enjoying life again, for the first time in many years. I wanted this relationship to continue and I wanted to see where it could go, even if parts of it scared me to death. I knew I had my own uncertainties about the possibility for stability or a future with the organization after me, but hopefully that could be worked out and the end result would allow me to stay there with my boys.

For the first time in forever, I had hope.

I climbed off the bed as I spoke in a whisper. "Almost broke me on that one."

Max gave a soft chuckle as he slowly got up off the bed. I watched as he covered Travis with a blanket before I turned and strolled into the bathroom to get cleaned up. Max came in behind me, sliding past me with a quick caress over my ass, and he started the shower. Without even needing words we both moved into the shower to get cleaned up.

"What do we do about Baxter?" Max

asked.

We hadn't had the chance to discuss Baxter and that whole situation yet. We had been having sex and sleeping since learning who was after Travis. I was still surprised that it was Baxter who had been abusing him. I knew of Baxter from the stories that I had heard and I knew he was homophobic. I just hadn't expected for him to be in the closet.

I knew that some guys, who were filled with so much self-hate that they were gay, turned violent toward others. That wasn't new to me. I had seen it, had investigated crimes in the past where it was a hate crime. I just hadn't pegged Baxter as one of those guys. He hid it well. Almost perfectly, in fact. He had it figured out down to the last detail. I knew that likely meant he had done the same type of thing before. Travis was not his first victim. That didn't mean the others were dead, Baxter could have easily abused them and allowed them to leave, but I wouldn't put it past him to have killed people and hidden the bodies, either. The man was dangerous and I wouldn't be neglecting that tidbit of information.

When someone like Baxter first started to date, they didn't always want to hold onto their victim. Abusers tend to build up over time. They start off slow and they see how far they can push things. It was a lot like a serial killer. They start off slow with animals and then they build up.

Abusers typically had previous victims who were able to get away only because the abuse wasn't as bad as their present victims. They may have been controlled and hit a few times, but they got away. Their abuser wasn't trying to keep a death grip on them.

As the abuser becomes more comfortable and gains self-confidence in being able to push their victim to a whole new level, the abuse becomes worse and their grip on their victim will increase and become tighter.

Now Travis was Baxter's most recent victim and had been for several years. He wasn't about to let him go. Baxter following him to Baton Rouge made that very clear. He was calling him, sending him photos, and now, he had destroyed Tavis' apartment and left a death photo. The situation was getting highly dangerous.

I suspected some of that escalation was due to myself and Max entering the picture, too. If there was one thing an abuser hated, it was their victim finding someone else. It didn't matter if Baxter believed we were all sleeping together or not. Just the fact that we were in Travis' life and we saw each other often, that was enough for Baxter to label us as a danger to him. It was probably why he had been going harder on Travis. He needed to prove he was still in control. He needed to break him. He needed Travis to feel like he had to leave town to keep us safe, leaving him alone and defenseless, and that is when Baxter would attack him and most likely kill him. That wasn't something that either Max or I were going to allow to happen. We needed to end this man's toxic, stalking behavior, and we had to do it fast before Baxter grew more angry and dangerous.

"We gotta find him. He's in the city so he has to be checked into a hotel somewhere."

"And when we do find him? Then what?" Max asked as we switched spots so I could be under the hot water.

What we did with Baxter, that was the million dollar question. He was a cop, an active cop, so it wasn't like we could just threaten him and move on. Baxter wasn't going to risk his career by allowing Travis to live. He had to kill him to ensure that Travis didn't talk.

I suspected that his previous victims weren't upstanding members of society. If Travis talked, people would listen. He was someone that people respected. He was a Social Worker; he wasn't some drug user or shady person who could be trying to maliciously bring down a good cop. People would listen if he spoke up and Baxter knew that. He wasn't going to risk that happening so he had to kill him. He had to make it look like either Travis fled town, or he was killed in a home invasion. There really was only one thing we could do.

"We kill him."

I could see the shock flash through his eyes at my simple statement. Between the two of us, I was the one always telling Max that he couldn't be a vigilante and kill people. I was the one who was always telling him that he needed to use his skills for good, but in a different way. In a way where it didn't put him at risk of getting killed or going to jail for the rest of his life. I knew he wanted to kill Baxter, but he hadn't been expecting me to agree and to say that we needed to kill an active cop. It would make things messy, I knew that, but I also knew we could cover it up.

Hell, we had done it before.

In a typical situation, I would suggest we needed to get Travis to file a report and press charges against Baxter. However, this wasn't a typical situation. Baxter was a cop and despite the fact that people would more than likely believe Travis' story, that didn't change that Baxter *was* a cop. He had connections that would keep him out of jail.

We had no solid evidence that what had happened in Baton Rouge was him. We also had no evidence that Baxter had ever hurt Travis. We didn't have any photos or scientific evidence that we could use to prove that Baxter was the one who had abused Travis. Everything we had was circumstantial and would leave way too much on the table as 'he said, he said.'

I also knew that having to testify was terrifying and I didn't think Travis would have it in him. That didn't mean I thought he was weak or incapable of being strong. I just knew that it wasn't easy to sit in an open court and look at someone to testify against them.

It had been hard for me and Sebastian to do it, and we hadn't been physically abused for years by the person sitting at that table across from us.

Travis would have to sit in an open court and look at Baxter, feel the man's hate-filled eyes on him the entire time, and tell people about the abuse the man had put him through. And then, he would have to deal with Baxter's lawyer trying to make it seem like he was lying.

It was why most cases for abuse didn't go anywhere. The victim can't handle the trauma of testifying and defense lawyers were all assholes. They only cared about getting their client off from the crime and not what they were doing to destroy the victim.

When Sebastian and I had testified, Russo's lawyers, all five of them, had tried to make it seem like we were mentally unstable. They wanted us to be evaluated by multiple shrinks; they wanted to plead that we were too incompetent for anything we had to say to be taken seriously. It didn't work, but it made a horrible situation even worse. It prolonged our pain, and that was the last thing I wanted for Travis.

"You see the irony in that, right?" Max asked with a smirk.

"Yeah, I know. But you know just as well as I do that he's too dangerous to leave alive. He's not going to stop until Travis is dead. Even if we could get him arrested, you know he's never going to see the inside of a jail cell. He'll use his connections to get out on bail and then he'll do everything he can to make it seem like Travis is unstable. He'll ruin his reputation and his career. The only way to save Travis, to protect him, is to kill Baxter."

"Hey, I'm not saying no. We find where he's staying, I can grab my rifle and take him out."

"Let's find him first before we start making execution plans. First step is finding this asshole."

I wasn't certain assassinating Baxter was the best route to go with this one. I wanted him dead, we needed him dead, but it might be better if it was a mechanical malfunction on his car, versus a bullet between the eyes. A clear hit would have every cop in the city on the hunt for whoever had done it. If he died in a car accident, then it could be ruled as an accident, or mechanical error, and that would be the end of it. We needed to kill him in the right way so it wouldn't come back on either of us or on Travis.

"Fine, just so long as the end result is the same, I'm good," Max said with a shrug before he leaned in and pressed his lips against mine. He kept the kiss quick before he slid out from under the water and climbed out of the shower and I let out a soft sigh.

How the hell had we gotten here?

***

It was nearing one in the afternoon when Travis finally made his way down the stairs. He had been asleep the whole time since our last intimate encounter and I could tell he had desperately needed the rest. He was freshly showered and he looked awake and perky for the first time in a long time.

Max and I had been spending the last few hours trying to track down Baxter. We had been running his name against all hotel and motel registrations in the city. We hadn't found him yet and it was becoming clear we were going to have a real problem figuring out where he was. He could be using a false name for the booking. He could also be at one of the motels that didn't keep their registration list online. Some didn't even care to grab a name if you paid in cash. We were going to have to physically go to the hotels and motels with a photo of him and see if we could find where he was staying. It was going to take longer, and that wasn't something either of us were happy about.

We also had to take into account if he was planning on staying here for longer than a couple of weeks, he could be renting an apartment or a house. There were plenty of short term rentals in the city, and he could have grabbed any of them and we wouldn't know which one. There was no database for short term rentals.

It wasn't like Baxter would need to update his government ID with the new address. He must have a car, but again, we couldn't find any rentals with his name. So, either he was driving his own vehicle, which would make sense, or he was using a false name for the rental. I suspected he was driving his own car so there wouldn't be a need for him to rent one. It would just add to his own complications and it would be hard for him to explain it away if he got arrested.

"He lives," Max quipped with a warm smirk.

"Sorry about falling back asleep," Travis said bashfully, with a shy smile crossing his lips as he looked at the ground.

"It's okay. You obviously needed the sleep. How are you feeling?" I asked.

He still didn't look too good. Not the way I figured he should after getting a good rest. He didn't look as tired as he did last night, but I could tell he was still rundown. He needed some food and some love to get back to being fully healthy.

"I'm okay. I guess I owe you both an explanation," he said slightly awkwardly, toeing the floor.

"You don't owe us anything, Sweetheart. But if you want to share, we will always be there to listen," I said as I held my hand out, indicating he should sit on the couch.

I could see him hesitate for a moment before he went over and plopped down on the couch. We both joined him, once again sitting on either side of him to show our support. We could both tell that Travis needed more support, more displays of affection than either of us needed. He had been abused, but I knew strong and confident people didn't tend to get abused. If they entered an abusive relationship, they left that first time they were hit. People who had lower self-esteem and self-confidence tended to be the ones who hung around and believed the lies and hope that things would turn around.

"What's going on, Sweetheart?" Max asked as he placed his hand on Travis' knee.

Travis sucked in a deep breath before he spoke. "I have a protein deficiency. It's idiopathic, so there's no real reason for my body to not absorb enough protein. But the lack of protein makes me tire easily, and I have a harder time gaining weight and healing. I also tend to get sick often from it."

"Do you take supplements?" I asked.

A protein deficiency wasn't what I had been expecting, but it did explain why he was so thin and always seems to fall asleep after sex. It also would explain why his bruises were still not fully healed even after a few weeks. I had never heard of a protein deficiency, but I did know that everyone's body needed protein to function properly.

"No. Your body can only absorb so much and with mine not absorbing the proper amount of protein, taking a supplement would be pointless. I basically have to eat healthy to try and keep my immune system up and to make sure my body gets all the nutrients that it needs. I would understand if you didn't want to keep being with me."

What the hell?

"I know I can speak for the both of us when I tell you that you having a medical condition, it's not a deal breaker, Sweetheart," Max said before I even had the chance to speak.

I couldn't believe Travis actually thought we wouldn't want to be with him because he had a medical condition. That would be like Travis and myself not wanting to be with Max because he had PTSD from his childhood trauma. We couldn't help having medical conditions, for fuck's sake; they were out of our control and not something anyone asks for. It was clear, though, that he had truly expected for us to not want to be with him because of it, and that made me believe that for previous boyfriends, even before Baxter, this had been an issue for them. Travis really hasn't dated anyone who was a good man and knew how special he was. How to treat him right, the way he deserved to be treated.

"I get sick a lot and I'm tired most of

the day. I can't play sports or do anything crazy active," Travis started, but I cut him off. I was not going to listen to him try and give us reasons as to why he didn't deserve to be with us.

"We don't care about that. We care about *you*, Sweetheart. We're not going anywhere. We all have problems, scars that we'll carry for the rest of our lives. It's part of who we are and I know neither one of you would walk away because of my own issues. Just like we wouldn't walk away from Max's issues. And trust me, he's got a few," I said, flashing a warm smirk at Max.

"Asshole," Max said, flashing a grin back at me before he looked at Travis again. "He's right. We all have baggage and we all have quirks. Your medical condition, it doesn't change how we feel about you and it never will. If you get sick, we'll take care of you. As for sports, neither one of us plays any and we can always make sure you get enough sleep after sex. We're not walking away, Sweetheart, so you better get used to having people in your corner."

I could see the tears building behind Travis' eyes. He hadn't expected for us to be on his side with this. He was going to need a lot of love and affection before he would be fully healed from all of the pain people in his life had caused him. We were both determined to make sure he was cared for. That he was healed from all of the abuse in his life. He was a good man and he didn't deserve any of this. He deserved the world and we were going to give it to him.

"Why don't I make us all something to

eat. Then afterward, you should go with Max to your hotel room and grab your things. I'll keep looking for Baxter," I suggested.

Travis just gave a nod in agreement and I knew he still needed some time to process everything that had happened. He would be going through a lot of emotions before this was all said and done, but we would get him through it. We would get him safe and then we would get him healthy and happy. We just needed to kill Baxter first.

CHAPTER EIGHTEEN

Max

WE PULLED UP to Travis' apartment building and nudged the car into a parking space.

We had already gone to his hotel room and grabbed his things and checked him out. I wanted to come to his apartment, though, for two reasons. One, I wanted to make sure he got everything that he wanted or needed that he couldn't grab when he ran. And two, I wanted to see the destruction with my own eyes.

Travis had said he hadn't cleaned up that night and he hadn't been back since. I didn't blame him for not spending the time to clean up. He was terrified and he had no idea if Baxter would come back that night. The smartest thing he could have done was run and worry about the mess later. I was already sure he would be losing his security deposit. I would need to talk to his landlord and see if there was something we could do. Hopefully, he would understand the situation and not use it against Travis. It would all depend on the type of landlord they were.

As I followed Travis up to his apartment, I was already getting a bad feeling about this place. It wasn't a nice place. The apartment building was rundown and dirty. The elevator didn't work, and even if it did I doubted I would be going into it. It looked like it was just one bad jerk away from collapsing.

Travis unlocked his door and we headed inside. Instantly, I could see the destruction that Baxter had caused. He didn't leave a single spot undamaged. Shit, the floor was even covered in paint. There was a great deal of hatred in this apartment. If Travis had been here, it could be his blood all over the floor instead of paint.

It was not lost on me that the apartment itself was a shit hole before the destruction. It was a crack shack, which didn't make sense when he made decent money as a Social Worker. He didn't have a spouse, no kids, and his medical condition didn't require medication or medical treatments.

So where was all of his money going?

"It's pretty bad, I know," Travis said with complete understanding to his voice.

"You were lucky you weren't here," I said, but I could tell that Travis was well aware of that fact.

He turned and headed toward his bedroom and I followed behind him. His room was a whole new level of disturbing. It was set up for a romantic evening, but for Baxter it would be a romantic evening of slowly killing Travis. There would be no love in this room. And once again, I couldn't help but notice the single bed, the old furniture. It screamed someone who didn't have much money.

"I have to ask, and I know it's a

personal question so feel free to tell me to fuck off. Where is your money going?"

I could see the understanding in his face before he answered. "Baxter. He took out loans in my name. He gambles and he loses all the time. I'm still paying off the loans. I don't really have much by the end of the month. Having the hotel for the past couple of days has maxed out my credit card. I was gonna have to come back here today or live in my car. There's one loan left, but it's high, it's really high. The interest rate is killing me. He got it from some loan shark; it's thirty-seven percent interest on a fifty thousand dollar loan. I'm gonna have to find a part-time job just to be able to afford food at this point."

He sounded so defeated and tired, just exhausted. He had been doing this for years now and on top of the abuse and fear, he'd had to deal with the financial strain that Baxter had placed on him. It was no wonder he was living in a place like this; he couldn't afford anything else.

Now I *really* wanted to kill the bastard.

I went over and joined him and placed my hand on the side of his face, cupping his cheek in my palm, my thumb scraping over the barest hint of five o'clock shadow.

"You can stay with me as long as you want. We'll figure it out, Sweetheart. First, is getting you safe. Afterward, we can figure out the financial aspect of this whole mess. It'll be okay, Sweetheart," I said, flashing him a warm smile and then pressing my mouth to his warm lips in a quick peck.

He offered me a small smile when I

pulled back and I knew it was going to take more than a few words to make him feel better. All we could do, though, was take this one step at a time and get him safe. Once we had Baxter in the ground, then we could work on figuring out how to help him with the illegal loan against his name.

I leaned in and placed another soft and quick kiss to his lips, then pressed my forehead to his. I didn't want to push him right now and I didn't want to get too caught up in loving on him. Not in this apartment. We could always have fun later. Right now, we needed to grab whatever he had left behind and then get back to my place where he would be safe.

I pulled back and I was instantly missing the connection to him. A quick look into his eyes told me he was feeling the same way.

"Come on, let's grab what you need and then get back to our man," I said, flashing him another a warm smile.

"I'd like that," he said, with a genuine smile turning up the corners of his lips.

That single legitimate smile told me everything I needed to know. He did like both Damien and myself. He liked being with the both of us, and knowing that had me feeling all bubbly. We would need to have a conversation about that today. If we were going to give it a real try, then we all needed to be on the same page.

I just hoped we could work it out. I knew having a three-way relationship was not going to be easy. We were going to have a lot we needed to figure out, and that was before we factored in how our friends and people in society would handle it. All of that could be worked out later, though. Right now, all that mattered was that we were together and we would all be safe.

***

We arrived back at my house and Damien was there to greet us outside. He helped us unload the car and bring Travis' items into my home. We had another load to bring in and my eyes picked up on the black four door sedan that was parked just down the street from my house. I made sure to not look directly at it, because it had been following us since we left Travis' hotel. I suspected it was Baxter and he had been watching Travis' hotel just waiting for him to leave.

I shot my hand out and placed it on the back of Damien's neck, pulling him in for a quick kiss before I kissed along his neck beside his ear so I could speak to him.

"Black, four door sedan just down the street. He's been tailing us since we left the hotel."

Damien placed his hands on my ass and started to kiss along my neck. I knew he understood what I was doing. He needed to get a look and we needed to come up with a plan.

"That's Baxter, I've seen him around. So he'd obviously been sitting on the hotel and waiting for when Travis would leave. I'm thinking he's done waiting and wants to end this quickly. He must have to get back to Gaithersburg for his job soon."

"We need to end this and we can do it today. He's the angry type, if we piss him off enough, he'll storm right into my house looking for blood. I'd be willing to bet everything I have that he's got a gun."

"You want to use Travis as bait. Use all of us as bait. Get him so pissed off he storms in and tries to kill us. If we do that, we would have to be ready for it. And we have to make sure Travis is on board."

I looked over and saw Travis walking back out. I pulled back slightly as I held my hand out for him. Travis easily took it and I pulled him so he was in between both Damien and me. Damien was instantly kissing along Travis' neck as I spoke.

"Baxter is here. He's in the black sedan just down the street from here. He's been following us since the hotel."

"Oh my god," he whimpered and I could see that he was about to freak out, but we needed to keep him calm so Baxter didn't know we were onto him.

"Stay calm. He can't know that we know he's here," Damien said as he ran his hand down the front of Travis' chest.

"We have a plan on a way to get rid of him. And I'm talking for good, Sweetheart. He could be dead within the hour and you will be free from him forever. But we need to know if that is what you want. Do you want him dead or we can arrest him and press charges against him for domestic abuse and allow the courts to handle it. The choice is yours and we will support you one hundred percent," I explained.

"We don't have enough for court," he said as he did his best to keep the expression on his face even.

With him being a Social Worker, he knew what we needed to make any of it stick within a courtroom and we didn't have anything we needed. And even if we did, Baxter's lawyers would be able to fight against it. There was a very high possibility that Baxter would be back out on the street within forty-eight hours.

"No, we don't. But if you don't want him dead, then that is what we will do," I said.

"I can't do this forever. I can't be afraid all the time. I can't be looking over my shoulder everywhere I go or too scared to fall asleep. I can't live this way," he said, with a deep amount of pain lacing his voice.

"And that's okay. We understand that, Sweetheart. We can end it today, but we need your help. I will handle killing him, but we need your help to piss him off enough so that he breaks into Max's house," Damien said.

"How?" Travis asked, still unsure. At least he was willing to help.

"We need to make him extremely mad so he has no choice but to take action. The best way we can do that is by making him jealous. We stand here and make out for a bit before we head inside. We can go up to my bedroom. We'll have a gun and be ready for when he comes in. All you have to do is play along with us. We'll keep you safe," I promised.

I knew this was asking a lot from him. I hadn't been planning on including Travis in killing Baxter. Neither Damien nor myself wanted him to be involved in any of this, but the best chance we had of killing him and getting away with it was right now. If he broke into my home with a gun, we were well within our legal rights to kill him. It would be simple and we would never have to worry about someone digging into his death. But neither of us were going to put Travis in a position he wasn't comfortable being in. If he said no, then we would come up with a new plan.

Travis let out a shaky breath and we both knew he was thinking about it. We weren't putting him in the best position with this situation. We both would have loved for him to not be connected to any of this, but it truly was our best chance. It was asking him to help lure a man into my house to be killed, though. He would need to lie to the police about some of what happened here. We would have to make it seem like we didn't know Baxter had been following us. The rest could stay the same, but it was still asking him to lie. Now, we could make it so that one of the guys from the Agency came to take the report and to handle the body. That would give us some leeway and it might keep Travis out of this part of it. Still, it was asking a lot for him.

"Okay. I can't do this forever. I need it to end. If this is the best way, then okay. What do I need to do?" Travis asked, sounding more confident that I had a feeling he felt.

"Just play along. Don't look at him and just focus on us," I said, before I went in for a kiss.

We had to make this look very good. We had to piss him off so badly that he threw all logic and common sense right out the window. We needed him to break into my house and try to kill us.

I held Travis close against me as we kissed. I knew Damien would be kissing him and running his hands all over his body. After a moment, I pulled back and got down on my knees. The position we were in and the height of my vehicle would make it so that Baxter wouldn't see what I was doing, but he would know it.

"Pretend he's sucking your dick, Sweetheart," Damien said against Travis' neck.

I felt Travis place his hand on my head and he arched back and gave a long moan. Damien started to grind against Travis' ass and I knew they would both be hard even though we had an audience. I couldn't wait until later on tonight when we could all play together for real. I wanted to feel both of them against me once again.

I was starting to think I needed a bigger bed. My room was big enough to handle a king size bed and it would give us plenty of room to roll around in it.

We kept at the fake blow job for a few more minutes before Travis gave a deep moan and I stood up. I pulled Damien in for a kiss and we both grinded against Travis' body. We needed to make it very clear that the three of us were together. After a moment, we pulled back and then headed inside.

Once we were inside, I closed my door, but I didn't lock it. I wanted to make it easy for Baxter to come into my house. Now that we were inside, I could see the heat within Travis' eyes, but I could also see the worry. This was going to be the scary part, but we would get through this.

"Come on, let's get up into my room," I said as I took Travis' hand in mine.

I brought them both into my room and

Damien left the door partway open. I then went over to my bedside table and pulled out my gun. I placed it under the pillow so Damien would be able to grab it easily. He just had to make sure he was on the bed. I wanted to be the one to kill the asshole, but I knew it would be better coming from Damien. He was the one with the connection to Mason and Roland. Plus, if he did have to go down to the station for the kill, it was better that they didn't have me being investigated. I had a lot more kills than Damien did and the last thing any of us needed was one of those kills coming back to bite me in the ass.

The irony was not lost on me.

I knew Damien had said that one day I might live to regret the choice to be a vigilante and it seemed like that day had come. I never thought it would, but here I was afraid of going to jail and being away from my men. After this was over and done with, I would need to re-evaluate my stance on vigilantism.

"Okay, Sweetheart, we're gonna lie on the bed and wait until we can hear Baxter. We'll hear him come up the stairs and then you and Max will kiss and I will take Baxter out," Damien explained to Travis.

"He's not going to hurt you, I promise I won't allow it," I promised him.

"I know you won't. I know either of you won't," he said, fear still shining brightly behind his eyes.

I got him down onto the bed and I lay next to him. Damien was behind me and I knew he had his hand on the gun underneath my pillow.

DAMIEN

We didn't have to wait long.

I could hear my front door opening and I turned and started to kiss Travis who was lying on his back. I could feel that he was anxious and scared, not that I could blame him. I hated that he was here for this, but I was going to protect him and make sure he didn't have to see any of it. I could feel Damien against my back and his body was tense. He was ready to react the second he needed to.

"You fucking whore," Baxter seethed as he pushed the door open so fast it smacked against the wall.

I instantly pulled away from Travis and looked over to see Baxter standing in the doorway, his face crimson in anger, a gun in his hand pointed at the ground. I kept my hand on Travis' chest to keep him down, though. I didn't want him to make any sudden movement that would cause Baxter to fire. We just needed him to talk long enough for Damien to get the gun out from the pillow without Baxter noticing.

"Who the fuck are you and why the fuck are you in my house?" I demanded.

"You dirty whore. You left me for them? You left me so you can be a slut with not one but two men. If I had known you liked to be fucked by two men, I could have put your ass on the street corner and made money from you. At least then you would have been worth something instead of being a worthless piece of shit. Maybe you need two men, though. You always were shit in bed, could barely get me off. At least when you are sick and pathetic in bed all the time they can still get off with each other."

"I don't know who the fuck you are, but the last thing he is is worthless. As for the sex, he has no problem making either of us come. I guess that means it's your dick that doesn't work and not him. Or maybe he just needed a real man to show him what pleasure is. What it feels like to have a real, big, juicy, dick inside of him, compared to your pathetic mini dick that he's had to suffer through. It's no wonder you couldn't even get him hard," I said back with a cocky smirk.

I had no idea if Baxter had been able to make Travis aroused. I was assuming based on how responsive Travis' body was that Baxter hadn't been able to turn him on. The point in my words was to piss Baxter off even more. I wanted his attention on me. I wanted him so furious that he didn't even see the gun coming.

I was also not going to sit here and listen to him talk shit about Travis. He was a good man, a sweet and kind man, and I was not going to allow anyone to talk shit about him. I wasn't going to allow Baxter to use Travis' medical condition against him. It wasn't his fault that he tired easily or that his immune system was weaker. It could happen to anyone and he deserved to be taken care of. He deserved to be cherished and worshipped. Baxter had no idea what a treasure Travis was and he never would.

Baxter did exactly what I thought he would, he turned the gun toward me and before he even had the chance to fire, Damien had pulled the gun out. I grabbed Travis and turned him into me just as Damien fired and killed Baxter with a bullet between the eyes. It was all over in a split second, before the echo of the gun throughout the bedroom had even dissipated.

Baxter lay on the floor, his glassy eyes open and staring off into the abyss, his gun still in his hand.

I didn't want Travis to see the man dead. I had no idea if he had ever seen someone dead before, but if not, I wasn't going to let this be his first time. His whole body was trembling in my arms and I knew he was already going into shock.

"It's okay, Sweetheart. You're okay, we're all okay," I reassured as I held him close to my chest, my hand tracing up and down over his back.

I looked over and saw Damien checking Baxter's pulse, but we both knew he was dead. Fuck, the damn blood was never going to come out of my floor. It might be time to move after all of this. This house was always going to be temporary anyway until I found one that I wanted to spend time in. Now might be the perfect time to start looking for something that could work in the big picture of things.

"I'll call Mason, you get him downstairs," Damien ordered.

I gave a nod and scooped Travis up into my arms. He kept his face buried in my neck and I was thankful that I didn't have to try and maneuver him around the dead body to keep him from seeing it. I could feel a warm wetness against my shoulder and I knew he was crying. All of this was a lot for him to be dealing with so I wasn't all that surprised at the tears. He was finally getting to release all of the pain and fear from the last few years. He was finally free from the abuse of Baxter and it all needed to come out.

I sat down on the couch with him in my lap and I held him against my chest as he cried his heart out. I knew Damien would handle Baxter and Mason when he arrived. It was my job to take care of Travis and that was exactly what I would be doing. Nothing was more important than my man.

***

"Thank you, we appreciate you handling all of this," I said as I shook Mason's hand.

It had taken a couple of hours for Mason and the Coroner to finish up with Baxter's body. He was now out of my house and I was left with a blood stain that was going to be a bitch getting out of the floor.

"It's no problem. I'm glad he's safe. One down, and now one more to go. I'll see you around."

I knew he was talking about the organization hunting Damien and Sebastian. We would have to handle that next, but for tonight I would be taking care of my men. With Mason gone, I turned to give my two lovers my full attention.

"Okay, we're leaving," I said, and I could instantly see the confusion in both of their eyes.

"You do know we don't need to go on the run, right?" Damien asked, and I wasn't certain if he was being serious or not.

"After what happened here tonight,

and with the large blood pool soon to be stained, on my bedroom floor, now is the perfect time to go to a hotel. I vote for one with a hot tub in the room and a king size bed."

"I know just the place," Damien said as he held his hand out for Travis to take.

I could tell Travis was all too happy to get out of this place. We didn't grab anything; we just headed out. None of us looked back at the now dark house. We all climbed into Damien's truck and he took off for the hotel. He gave me the name and I easily pulled it up on my phone and booked us a suite on the penthouse floor with a double king size bed and a hot tub big enough for eight people in the room. It was perfect and exactly what we needed.

The second we arrived, we quickly

checked in and made our way to our room. It was just like the photos on the website and truly breathtaking. "Now this is a room," I said as I strolled over and turned on the hot tub.

"Come on, Sweetheart, let's relax and wash the day away," Damien said as he went and helped Travis to get undressed.

I opened the mini-fridge, snagged a few small dark brown colored bottles from the shelf, and made us all a stiff drink. We could all use some whiskey after the hell we'd dealt with today.

Once we were all situated in the hot tub, with Travis between us, I spoke.

"How are you feeling, Sweetheart?"

"I don't know yet. Numb. None of this even feels real just yet."

Travis had been in shock for a good few hours over what happened with

Baxter. Both Damien and I hated that he had to be involved in this, but it had been our best chance of killing Baxter and getting away clean from it. I was just hoping that he would be able to process all of this and be okay with it, be okay with us for making that decision.

"It'll take some time, but you will process it. We're sorry that you had to be involved in that," Damien said, trailing his fingertips over Travis' arm.

"I understand why it had to be done that way. I'm not upset that he's dead. Underneath the shock, I do feel relieved and free. I think it's just going to take a little bit for my mind to process everything and get used to a normal life now. What happens to us now?"

"Well, that depends on what we all want, I guess. I would love to be with you both. I know it's unconventional and I am sure there will be problems that come up along the way, but I would like to give this a real shot," I admitted.

I was hoping they both wanted that as well. I knew it wasn't going to be easy for any of us and we were going to have to navigate through a whole new territory for the three of us, but I wanted to try. I wanted to have them both in my life.

"It's not going to be easy, but I can't imagine my life without both of you in it," Damien agreed.

"I want that, too. Though, I'm not really sure how it will work," Travis added.

"We can figure it out. We have lots of time to figure all of it out. What matters is that we all want to be together," I said, flashing them both a warm smile.

It warmed my heart to hear that they both wanted the same future I did. That they both wanted to see where this thing between us could go. I was worried that they may not have wanted to make our relationship into something serious, that they just wanted to have some fun and nothing more, so the relief I felt in that moment was extraordinary. Knowing that they wanted to give our relationship a real chance, I couldn't have been happier.

"We'll figure it out, but we don't have to do that tonight. Tonight, let's relax and enjoy each other's company. I know of a few ways we can pass the time that will help us all feel so much better," Damien said, flashing a grin and a wink at both of us.

And that was exactly what we were going to do.

EPILOGUE

Travis

Four Months Later…

"ARE YOU GUYS ready? We can't be late." I called out to my men.

We were getting ready to head out for Finley's and Rafe's wedding. They had gotten engaged close to a year ago and today was their big day. Everyone in the Agency was going to be there for it, and then afterward, we would be going to their home for the reception and party. They were having a simple wedding with just close family and friends. It was a gorgeous summer day and I knew it was going to be a great day for everyone.

I was very happy and excited for both Finley and Rafe, they were truly soulmates and I couldn't have been more in awe of the love they had for each other and for Lilly. Watching them together, as a family, convinced me that was what I, too, wanted some day. A family to call my own.

Lilly was very excited for her flower girl duties today, and I knew she would steal the show. The little girl had adjusted remarkably well since being kidnapped and held in a child sex trafficking ring for almost two years. We couldn't see the fear and trauma in her eyes anymore, and though we all knew she was still going to have problems from time to time, she was back to being a happy and healthy little girl.

Rafe and Fin were still keeping her in therapy, but it was only once a week for an hour. They wanted to make sure nothing snuck up on her. She was doing extremely well with her service dog, Pepper, too. Clearly getting her the dog had been the perfect decision. They were good men and I was so happy for them all.

"We're waiting on you, Sweetheart," Max said as came up behind me and placed a kiss on my cheek.

"I'm ready," I said, flashing a warm smile into the mirror at him as I finished fixing my tie.

Looking back, I still couldn't believe my life had changed as much as it had. Just last year, I never thought I would be free from Baxter and his abuse, but now, I was in a happy and healthy relationship with not just one, but *two* incredible and loving men.

Baxter's death had been ruled as self-defense and I was very relieved that Damien hadn't been charged with his murder. Only the three of us knew what we had done, that we had baited and lured him into the house so Damien could kill him. I knew it had been wrong, but I really couldn't have imagined any another way to handle him. I couldn't have gone through the court system. It wouldn't have worked to begin with. He would never have been arrested and he would have continued to stalk me and eventually, he would have killed me. It was either him or me, and I did what I had to do, what everyone would do, I chose my own life over his.

When Max, Damien and I had decided to give this thing between the three of us a real shot, I wasn't too confident that it would work out. I thought for sure that we would be jealous of each other, or that one of us would inevitably feel left out, but we had made it work. Even when I would walk in on them kissing, I never felt any jealousy, I felt turned on, and they always welcomed me with open arms.

We had come up with a few simple rules, one of which was that we could do anything sexual with each other, but we had to tell each other everything. There were no secrets between us in or out of the bedroom. Ever.

One night, over a bottle of whiskey and pizza, we had all opened up to each other. I told them everything about Baxter and my parents. Max had told me the horror of his childhood with his father. Damien had informed me about the Italian Mob being after him and his brother, and not best friend, Sebastian. It was a lot for me to take in, but I needed to hear it all. I needed to know who these men were just as badly as they needed to know who I was.

That evening had brought us all closer.

We had also decided that we weren't going to hide our relationship from the people in our lives. With my apartment being a wreck, and Max wanting to move due to the blood stain in his bedroom, not to mention the bad memories the place now held, we had all stayed at Damien's place. Sebastian still lived there, but he was good with his brother being happy dating two men, thankfully.

All of our friends were thrilled for us and that was something that still shocked me to no end. I had honestly figured that they would have made disparaging comments and been disgusted with our decision to be in a three-way relationship. It wasn't, after all, a societal norm to date more than one person at the same time. I mean, there were laws against marrying more than one person. I knew we would never be able to get married, at least not legally, but that didn't matter to me. We all loved each other and that was all that truly mattered.

We had moved into a new house together just two weeks ago. Our house. We had invested in a double king size bed and it was more than worth every penny we spent on it. We spent the night breaking it in and it was glorious. We were all having fun and enjoying each other. We had created a real functioning relationship despite all odds that we would never work out. We had created a home and I couldn't have been happier. I had no idea my life could even be this blissful. I didn't think it was possible, but here I was.

I was loving my job. I'd become a huge part of the Social Services department in Baton Rouge and we were helping children by the handful every single week and nothing thrilled me more than seeing the *real* smiles on their faces as I went to the foster homes for my monthly check-ins. My life was good. For the first time in I didn't even know how long, I was happy and excited to start each day.

The safe haven homes had been chosen and the repair funding approved by the city and private investors who were getting a tax write off. Construction had begun and on Monday, I would be starting the process of selecting people to run them. We were getting somewhere with the project, though, and I knew that these homes were going to be a huge step in the right direction for at-risk kids. Hopefully, we would be able to keep them safe this time and we wouldn't have a repeat of the last safe haven home.

"Let's go, you two, we got a wedding to get to," Damien said, interrupting my thoughts with a warm kiss on my cheek.

"You got the wedding gift?" I asked as we headed out of the bedroom.

"I got it, plus Lilly's gift," Max said as

he grabbed the two colorful gift bags.

We strolled out and climbed into Damien's truck. He turned the key and the beast started with a roar and a vibrating rumble I could feel in the cushioned seat. He shifted the vehicle smoothly into gear and we started off for the wedding.

We had picked up a gift for Lilly to make her feel like she was a real part of the wedding. Everyone had also been spoiling her because of what she had been through. She was such a sweet little girl it was so hard to imagine anyone trying to hurt her. She had lost her parents, but she now had a lot of overprotective uncles in her life to be there for her.

It was so surreal that I was now a member of that family. That I had all of these strong and powerful men, good-hearted, loving men, in my life. I had come from an extremely small family of just my parents and me. A family with no love. And now, I had this enormous family with all of this real and unconditional love, and it was all because of Damien and Max. They had given me the love of a family and the love of two soulmates. I knew some would argue that you couldn't have two soulmates, but I didn't believe that. I think our souls belonged to each other, that our souls were meant to be connected to each other, and it wasn't anyone's business to dissect it or judge us. We were happy and I wouldn't have my life any other way.

"Maybe one day we will be going to our own wedding," Max said, his voice slightly wistful.

"It wouldn't be legal," Damien pointed out.

"No, but people get married spiritually over a legal one. We could marry that way. I'm not proposing or anything, I'm just saying that one day maybe it'll be us who are getting married," Max explained.

"I'd like that," I said with a big smile turning up the corners of my lips.

I didn't care if it was legal or not. I would love to marry them both one day. I would love to stand in front of our family and friends and share our love with them all. I didn't know what we would do about last names, but that was part of the fun, part of the adventure the three of us were going on.

I hated that the only reason we even got to start this adventure was because of Baxter, though I tried not to let that taint it. If I hadn't been dating him, then I wouldn't have had a reason to make the move down to Baton Rouge. I never would have left Gaithersburg and that meant I would never have met Damien and Max. As much as I hated Baxter, and I was glad he was dead, if I hadn't been with him, I never would have gotten the chance to fall in love with my men.

Now, I never wanted to lose them.

Baxter thought he would be the one to destroy me, that he would kill me, but in the end, because of him, I got to be saved. Because of him, I got to experience what true love felt like and because of that, I had forgiven him for everything he had put me through. I didn't need to live with that kind of hate in my heart. I wanted to spend my life with pure love in my heart and there was no room for Baxter in my life anymore in any way, shape, or form.

"You got your hand sanitizer?" Damien asked as he parked his truck in the lot at the wedding ceremony.

"Yes, it's in my pocket. I swear, you both worry too much," I said, flashing them a loving smile.

They had been very good with my medical condition and the fact that I was often tired and got sick every month. Whenever I got sick, though, they were both there to take care of me. Whenever I got home from a long day at work and fell asleep on the couch, one of them would carry me up to bed. They never got upset with me, they just loved me in every way possible, and it meant the world to me.

"You have to be careful, you just got over pneumonia," Damien said.

"And we would both really like to see

how many times we can make you come tonight," Max added with that devilish smirk of his plastered over his mouth.

"Oh well, in that case I will make sure to use it all day," I said with a big smile turning up the corners of my mouth.

I was more than looking forward to spending time with them tonight. I was looking forward to spending time with them *every night* for the rest of our lives. I had found my soulmates and I was finally, truly, happy.

Thank you for reading Damien, the sixth book in the Federal Protection Agency. Read Sebastian now!
If you enjoyed this book, please leave me a review, and hey, don't forget to tell all your friends about the FPA!
~Love, Evie.

As you've no doubt figured out, all of my contemporary gay male romance books so far can be read standalone, but they are truly best if read in order if you prefer to know the back story of their family and friends. There are several instances of this kind of cross over in From the Edge and Federal Protection Agency, and that will likely continue through Smokejumpers where we will introduce more delicious men who live for nothing more that to help others, even when it puts them in the way of danger.

My next series, Smokejumpers, may feature some of the men you've already come to know and love from FTE and FPA, so look for Book One, Hawke, at your favorite online retailer!

In the meantime, why not check out another one of my series, the Gray Vale Pack, a wolf shifter paranormal romance, with a preview of His Fated Mate on the next page.

Enjoy!

PREVIEW

CONALL

THE FOREST AROUND us radiated life. I drank it in through nose and ears, but there was so more to it than that. My wolf growled inside me, sensing prey.

The feeling was so strong that even my human side itched for action. Any excuse to shift would be fine by me. Patrolling this disputed region between our lands and Stoke

Ridge only tossed me a little excitement once in a while, but today felt rich with potential.

Glen came up beside me. The prickling of energy coming off him only got me even more keyed up.

"Deer," I murmured.

"Duh," Glen replied. "You're not the only one with a fuckin' nose, Connie."

I reached out and slapped the back of his head without even looking. "What've I told you about calling me that?"

Glen let out a low growl. "Used to let me."

"That was when I was also fucking you. You see the connection there, dude?"

Immediately, our attention flew across to the clearing, and the big buck that crept into sight.

Glen slid his rifle down off his shoulder, but I stopped him.

"Uh-uh. We do it like nature intended."

"Ugh, seriously? That's one thing I

definitely don't miss about you."

I stripped off in seconds, fending away Glen's lustful glare as I did. We'd had our chance, and it didn't work out. If he couldn't get over it then he was no good as a member of my patrol.

He kept his voice low and deep. "Why do you even come out with us lowly shit-kickers, anyway, Conall? You have options guys like me could never even dream of."

"You call going to fancy-pants shindigs and week-long meetings *options*? That's not me, bro. Besides, in three days, my sister is taking the fall for all of us."

That was the biggest downside to being what amounted to pack royalty. Marriages and matings that were all about strategy. Thankfully, that shit didn't apply to me. Only hetero pairings were recognized, still.

Because of all that, my twin, Fiona, was gonna be all hitched up to the pristine, primped and puckered heir of the Stoke Ridge Pack, Zoltan Valenta. And all for the lamest of reasons.

Peace.

More like death, as I saw it. If we couldn't get into harmless little pissing contests with our snobbish neighbors, then what the hell was the good of being wolves? Life is conflict, and vice versa.

I glanced across at Glen. "You're still dressed."

"C'mon, Con. You know how your father is."

Yeah, I knew. He treated shifting like it was a religious ceremony. Just like the ancient ones had. Tradition was everything in wolf packs.

"Dude, if my father's fancy notions mattered to me, I wouldn't be out here with you lowly shit-kickers, now. Would I? I'd be lying back on a fucking velvet sofa with servant boys feeding me grapes."

Glen made a quiet scoffing sound and worked his clothes off. "Let's just fucking get this done, so I don't have to hear any more shit."

I shook my head with a wry smile. "Do you even shift, bro?"

Before he'd finished rolling his eyes, I opened myself up to the wolf, letting it ignite within me. Shifting was like sex. No matter how many times I did it, I always wanted more.

My body jolted, my muscles and bones danced around each other, and then it was done. I didn't even wait for Glen. The scent of that buck was too fucking delicious.

I crept forward, keeping low. The buck was spooked already. It was a buzz in the air that brought his scent with it. Twenty feet. Fifteen. His big body quivered and he cast his head around. No need to run this guy down. He was so close I could almost taste him.

As I tensed to spring at my prey, a rifle shot rang out. The assault of noise had me flinching away, and a second later the buck dropped dead.

I'd been so close. Glen was gonna pay for that. Robbing my wolf of his succor. In my rage, I shifted back, ready to tear my cohort a new one.

Before I could turn around, three men in Stoke Ridge uniforms moved into the clearing from the far side. One of them carrying a rifle, all of them pleased with themselves. Obviously new recruits, or they'd be treading a lot more carefully.

I marched forward, more than ready to turn my anger on them. I sensed, rather than saw, Glen moving into position behind me.

"Hey! You fuckin' Stoke Ridge assholes."

All three of the other side's patrolmen tensed as we moved closer. "Back down, Gray

Vale. It's our trophy."

"Not when you bag it on our land."

Rifle dude sneered at me. "Well, when we bag one on your land, pal, we'll be sure to let you know. But this here is Stoke Ridge land."

I took a cleansing breath. As much as I'd been looking forward to taking down that buck, that would have been little more than an appetizer. This here was main course and dessert, all rolled into one. There was nothing I liked quite so much as tussling with these hoity-toity Ridgers.

"Is that right?"

"You know it is, grunt. Now, run off back to your kennels." He flicked his eyes down for a split second and then back up. "And tuck that tail of yours between your legs."

I gave the guy a flash of teeth. "Or maybe you want that... *tail*... right between *your* legs, Ridgy. I see how you look at me."

For me, that was just a throwaway

comment. But for a Ridgy, it was the ultimate slur. Stoke Ridge society was stuck in the fucking nineteenth century when it came to sexuality.

Okay, a taunt like that one was low-hanging fruit, but all I wanted was for them to make the first move. The fact it worked so well every single time only meant I'd keep using it again and again.

Rifle dude snarled and handed his weapon to his right hand man. I went into a crouch, arms out, waiting.

The guy burst forward, charging straight for me. Like a fucking amateur. I let him slam into me, chest to chest, before spinning on the spot and throwing him halfway across the clearing. He landed in a sprawling mess of limbs.

"Now, you guys stand down," I said, letting all my menace and breeding come bubbling out in my voice. It did no good, though. These guys were young, dumb and full of... themselves.

The rifle guy sprang up to a squat, baring his teeth, which were growing longer.

I raised one eyebrow. "You gonna take this down to wolf level, kid?" That was the other thing with Stoke Ridge. They were even more stuffy about shifting than my father was. "'Cause I spend half my life there. Do you?"

That gentle little reminder seemed to do the trick, and he came back up onto his feet. When he approached me this time, he showed a ton more caution. Still not enough, though.

He threw a wild punch that couldn't have been more telegraphed. It was like a movie punch. He spent so much time pulling his arm back I could have made a coffee while I waited for him to throw it.

I pulled my head back and let his fist fly past, then wrapped my hands around the back of his head and neck, throwing him into the scrub and dirt face first.

No other man had even moved yet. Glen leaned back on a tree, stifling a yawn. The Stoke Ridge guys looked wide eyed and shell shocked. I already knew they were green, but I wouldn't mind betting this was their first ever patrol. That'd explain why they were so cavalier about taking down the buck on disputed lands.

As the main Ridgy came back up onto his feet, I held my hands up for calm. "Give it up, dude. Take your lumps and head back home."

"I'll take my lumps. And my trophy."

"No, you'll be leaving the buck." I crossed my arms and narrowed my eyes. "Understood?"

I could see a thousand different words bubbling up in his head. Some of them were punching so hard at his pride he almost said them.

"All right," he ground out. "But you

understand *this*... I'm not backing down."

"No? It kinda looks like you are."

"Well, unlike you peasants, we here in Stoke Ridge value tradition. So, I'm allowing this to pass, for the sake of the upcoming wedding." He took his rifle back from his cohort and curled his lip. "You... do know about the wedding, right?"

"Of course he does," Glen interrupted. "He's—"

"I'm not interested in it. Perky prince Zoltan is lucky we're letting him into our pack at all."

The other guy tensed all over. I wasn't even sure he realized he'd tightened his grip on the weapon. "Let's be clear, you ass. It's your woman who's being elevated here. You and your caretaker Alpha should get on your knees and thank—"

That was as far as he got before my fist hit the side of his face. As much as I loved being wolf, sometimes hands worked better than paws.

The guy dropped like a sack of dirt, and I landed on him just as heavily. My weight on his chest, my hand on his throat.

His two patrolmen froze, their fear filling my nostrils. I'm sure they could sense the battle experience and silent aggression radiating off me, and made the sensible decision to stand down.

"Now it's your turn to listen, sunshine," I growled. "Yeah, Patrick Blair is only a second generation Alpha. If you think that weakens our pack in any way, you're welcome to test your claims."

"Get the hell off me. And for God's sake, cover yourself up."

"You Ridgies are so damn uptight. Never met a bunch of shifters so fuckin' scared of being naked." I rolled my hips just a little. "Or maybe you're scared of how much you're enjoying the view."

"Get off."

As much as I enjoyed roughing up Ridgies, this little scene had passed its sell-by date. There was nothing to be gained anymore. I stood, and offered the guy my hand. He slapped it away and got to his feet at his own speed.

"Lord Valenta will hear of this."

"Lord? You guys are so into this hierarchy shit it's... well, it's fucking embarrassing."

"Whether you accept it or not, every pack is a hierarchy, grunt. And the wrath of your Alpha will come down on you for this."

"It won't be the first time."

They turned and headed back into their territory with a last, narrow-eyed glare at the buck they'd taken down.

As they disappeared into the brush, another of my patrol team came running up from behind.

"Alec," I said. "What's up?"

"Better get dressed, dude. I'm taking your duties from here on. Daddy wants a word with you."

Glen chuckled without any real humor. "Wrath of the Alpha, indeed. News travels fast."

For more of Conall and Zoltan action, snag your copy of His Fated Mate at your favorite online retailer now!

OTHER BOOKS BY EVIE

Federal Protection Agency

Mason

Rafe

Ryzen

Cooper

Noah

Damien

Sebastian

Gabe

Logan

Ruthless Empire

Courting Danger

Chasing Danger

Kissing Danger

Smokejumpers

Hawke

Cyrus

Jase

Gage

Jackson

Xavier

Jasper Springs

Cade

Dawson

Drew

Grayson

Riley

Mitch

From The Edge

Shattered

Runaway

Jaded

Rescue

Hidden

Tormented

Gray Vale Pack

His Fated Mate

His Wounded Warrior

His Healing Heart

ABOUT THE AUTHOR

Evie Riley is a prolific, neurodivergent author known for her captivating MM romance novels. She has gained a significant following and topped the LGBT+ action and adventure bestseller charts with her series.

Evie's writing style often explores dark and gritty themes where her men must overcome difficult obstacles in their search for love, but she has also ventured into sweeter small-town romances, incorporating tropes like enemies-to-lovers, friends-to-lovers, age-gap, and forced proximity. She is known for crafting engaging romantic suspense novels and has a knack for creating interconnected series worlds that keep readers invested.

Interestingly, Ms. Riley has hinted at exploring new genres, such as Alien Omegaverse Romance, in the future.

Outside of writing, she enjoys spending time at the beach and has a quirky personality, described by her partner as ranging from cute to deadly, depending on her blood-chocolate levels.

Evie spends her nights writing bad boys in love, and her days wrangling the sweet boys she loves.